# THE
# CHRISTMAS
# PROMISE

RICHARD PAUL EVANS

# THE
# CHRISTMAS
# PROMISE

NEW YORK LONDON TORONTO SYDNEY NEW DELHI

Gallery Books
An Imprint of Simon & Schuster, Inc.
1230 Avenue of the Americas
New York, NY 10020

First Gallery Books hardcover edition November 2021

GALLERY BOOKS and colophon are registered trademarks of Simon & Schuster, Inc.

For information about special discounts for bulk purchases, please contact Simon &
Schuster Special Sales at 1-866-506-1949 or business@simonandschuster.com.

The Simon & Schuster Speakers Bureau can bring authors to your live event. For
more information or to book an event, contact the Simon & Schuster Speakers
Bureau at 1-866-248-3049 or visit our website at www.simonspeakers.com.

Interior design by Erika R. Genova

Manufactured in the United States of America

1   3   5   7   9   10   8   6   4   2

Library of Congress Cataloging-in-Publication Data has been applied for.

ISBN 978-1-9821-7742-3
ISBN 978-1-9821-7743-0 (ebook)

*To Allyson*
*(forever my Mowgli)*

# THE
# CHRISTMAS
# PROMISE

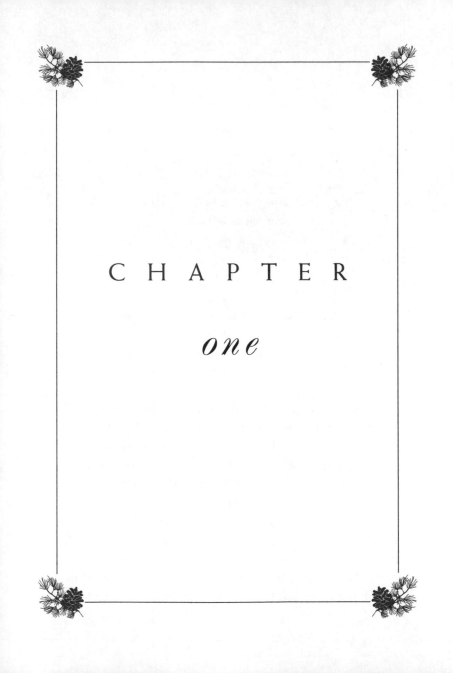

# CHAPTER

## *one*

*If a girl cries alone in her house and no one hears her,*
*does she make a sound?*
—*Richelle Bach's Diary*

Thinking back on that winter makes me feel cold. Maybe it *was* colder than usual. I remember there was an unusual polar front that glazed Salt Lake City in ice for a week. Still, I'm not sure if it was as cold as I remember or if I was just lonely.

I'm not being facetious. Psychologists have proven that loneliness makes people feel cold, which is why single people drink more coffee and take longer hot showers than those in relationships. My father told me that. He was always dropping random facts the way a wedding planner scatters rose petals. Trivia like "Oxford University is two hundred years older than the Aztec civilization" or "A cloud weighs more than a million pounds." That's what my childhood was like.

My father's name was Richard Bach, like the writer of that seagull book, but not him. I was close to my father. He was my hero. When he died the previous January, I felt like part of me was buried with him. I still do.

I had two deaths that year. The second loss was my identical twin sister, Michelle. It was summer when she died and that brought a whole different kind of cold. Most people assume that losing my twin was even harder than losing my father, but it wasn't. I had lost Michelle long before she died. My sister and I were estranged when she passed, and we hadn't spoken in more than six years. I was living alone in my father's home in Salt Lake City when I learned of her death from a stranger.

Peculiarly, I sensed the exact time of her death without knowing it. I was at work when I suddenly felt a sharp pang in my side so intense that I doubled over. Since I work at a hospital, I was quickly brought to the ER. The attending doctor thought it was a ruptured appendix, but it wasn't. In fact, the blood tests and scan showed nothing. What I didn't know until six days later was that, at that very moment, seven hundred miles away in California, my twin sister had been struck by a car.

Michelle had been riding her bike when a car driven by a drunk driver ran the light and hit her. I later learned that the impact had been on her right side below the ribs—exactly where I felt my pain. She was killed instantly. I've read that it's not possible that I felt something, that it was just a coincidence. I don't know. It's not like I could prove it. I'm just telling you what happened.

Like I said, I hadn't talked to Michelle for more than six years. The last thing I said to her I wish I could take back. It may have been true at the time, but I still regret saying it. No one wants their last words to someone to be something that hateful.

My name is Richelle, though my father always called me Ricki. My twin sister's name was Michelle, though those close to her called her Micki. Ricki and Micki. Our names were pretty much used interchangeably since no one could ever tell us apart. For most of my life, I answered to both.

Michelle was born just twelve minutes after me. We were frighteningly identical. Like zebras or penguins. Add to the equation that my mother was Taiwanese, so we had Asian features, and no one could tell us apart. If I had a dollar for every time I heard, "You Chinese all look alike," I'd hire a hit man. But it's not just an Asian phenomenon. There are studies that show that people have trouble distinguishing people of different races. To Chinese, white people all look alike, and so on. Another factoid courtesy of my father.

Correction: no one could ever tell my sister and me apart until they knew us. Our identicalness, if that's a word, was only skin deep. In personality we couldn't have been more different.

I didn't think Michelle's death would affect me as much as it did. But even apart we were connected in ways I still don't fully comprehend. Her death didn't end that. Like phantom limb syndrome, I could still feel pain from her. I suppose it didn't help that I saw her in the mirror every day. Even though I was only several minutes older than her, I had always felt protective of her. Even after she betrayed me.

If I were being totally honest, I'd take the blame for my loneliness. I sabotaged relationships the way a demolition team brought down buildings. I had my reasons. I could even argue they were good reasons, though that would be arguing that something bad was good. Then, that cold winter, all that changed in a way I couldn't have imagined. Actually, the thing I think of first when I think back on that winter isn't the cold. It's *him*. And how he changed everything.

> *My father once described hope as "the consolation of a weary traveler when the destination is still out of sight." At this point in my life, hope, I suppose, is the reason I get out of bed in the morning.*
> —*Richelle Bach's diary*

This story is true. In sharing it with you, I've included a few of the diary entries I wrote at that time in my life. Those short passages are truer glimpses into my journey than this book could ever be. That's because it's one thing to retell an event, but it's a whole different matter to walk it wearing the blindfold of uncertainty.

Knowing how a story ends may take away our fear, but in so doing, it must equally take away our hope. And to tell this story without hope would rob it not only of its truth but also of its deepest meaning.

If my story seems stranger than life, it's not my fault. A writer friend once said to me, "The difference between fiction and nonfiction is that fiction has to at least pretend to be true. Life isn't just stranger than you imagine, it's stranger than you *can* imagine."

Until the winter that this story took place—until I met *him*—I couldn't have known just how right he was.

# CHAPTER

*two*

*I read somewhere that the Bedouins believed that opals contained lightning and fell from the sky during thunderstorms. Maybe that's why I never take my pendant off—it subconsciously makes me feel powerful. It might also be why I keep having these dreams.*

—*Richelle Bach's diary*

For millennia, opals have enthralled and mystified humanity. They have been called the gem of royalty and also blamed for the fall of monarchies. While some claimed the gem brought good luck, others likened the stone to the evil eye, attracting ruin and evil. Some cultures believed the stone contained the spirits of the dead. During the Great Plague it was said the opal would lose its fire when its wearer died.

For more than a year I had a recurring dream about opals. A lucid dream—one of those where half the brain knows it's dreaming, while the other is lost in the illusion. The setting for my dream changed from time to time, but the premise was always the same. I was much younger in my dream than I am now, a girl of ten or eleven.

I'm standing alone in a large, open grassy field. The grass has gone to seed and is nearly to my knees. A warm wind ripples the grass.

In my hand there are two large black opals. The stones feel warm and I can feel them moving in my palm. From a distance they look identical, but on closer inspection the colors inside the stones are very different—one a crimson and orange, the other an incandescent purple and blue—both of the stones shimmering like fire. The gems grow hotter until I drop them in the grass. I immediately fall to my knees to find them but I can't. They're gone. That's where the dream would end, where I would wake, panting and out of breath.

I didn't know why I was having this dream, but I can guess why there were opals. Opals have significance in my life. They're Michelle's and my birthstone. The evening before Michelle and I graduated high school, my father gave both of us a necklace: a gold pendant with a black opal. The opals were almost a full karat, with smooth, round edges, like a pebble. My father presented them to us with a sort of ceremonial bequest. He told us that opals were prized by ancient royalty. "While I'm not superstitious," he said, "the black opal is the rarest of all opals and promised to bring good fortune"— something he hoped for both of us. Then he said, "But to me there's a deeper meaning. The opals look identical, but the fire inside each—the play of colors—is different. Just like the two of you. To those who don't know you, you appear identical. But you are individually unique. Not better, not worse. Both of you are priceless to me."

He added, almost as an afterthought, "You should know,

these gems were very expensive. They're part of your inheritance. I thought you might enjoy them more than a savings bond. What I'm saying is, you don't want to lose them." That's probably why I always woke in a panic.

Michelle and I both wore our necklaces to graduation, which no doubt added to our twinness. In our caps and gowns we looked even more alike. But our graduation-night experience couldn't have been more different. I was salutatorian, which meant I gave the opening speech of the ceremony. Michelle barely graduated. In fact, had I not stepped in to take one of her exams, she wouldn't have gotten a diploma that night.

What made that evening especially difficult for Michelle was that all night long people—mostly teachers and parents—congratulated her on my academic accomplishment and the speech I gave. When I went to hug her after the ceremony she wouldn't talk to me. That was the beginning of our great divorce. I went to dinner with my friends. Michelle ran off with hers to party.

From there, our paths continued to diverge. I worked that summer as a math tutor, then went on to college that fall, while Michelle, to my father's dismay, hitchhiked across Europe with a boy she barely knew. Literally, as well as figuratively, our paths never crossed again. Except once. And that was to end us once and for all.

# CHAPTER

*three*

*I'm not sure why nurses all wear Crocs, but we do. It's one of those inexplicable laws of nature—like anyone over seventy must move to Florida or Subaru owners must have a COEXIST bumper sticker.*
—*Richelle Bach's diary*

## FRIDAY, NOVEMBER 8

It was usually still dark in the morning when I got to the hospital. This was especially true in the winter, when the clouds added an extra blanket for the sun's slumber. I was used to starting work before the sunrise. This had been going on for a long time. I'd worked at Mountain Regional Hospital for six years and felt as much a fixture as the patient monitors and ventilators. I had been there longer than most of them.

One of the perks of my job was I never had trouble deciding what to wear, since I wore the same thing every day—the dark purple scrubs of a trauma nurse. While my uniform and daily routine were always the same, my workday never was.

Every day brought new drama, which is probably why there are so many television series based in hospitals.

The group of nurses I worked with on a daily basis changed every shift. It was like the constant shuffling of a deck of cards: every hand is different but you know all the cards.

The first thing I did when I got to work was log on to the computer and look over my daily assignments—which patients I had, which rooms I'd find them in. (Since I work in an Intensive Care Unit—an ICU—I rarely have more than two patients at a time.)

Then all the nurses on the shift gather in the breakroom for the morning "huddle," which is exactly what it sounds like. The charge nurse, our quarterback, gives us an update on the unit's flow, the rooms, patients, and staff, and generally what to expect for the day. She also keeps on us about our learning modules, which we are supposed to complete during our "downtime," which presupposes that there actually is downtime. There rarely was.

Afterward, I meet with the previous shift nurse whose rounds I'm taking over. She updates me on my patients, their medications, any new developments, and what kind of night the child had.

Then I start my rounds, visiting my patients. Sometimes they're new, sometimes we've already built a rapport. I talk to them, and the work continues, round and round. Sometimes I feel like Sisyphus, continually pushing that rock up that hill. There are constant details that need tending, with no room for error. Complex medication schedules, sepsis screening, drips, vent settings, drain outputs and measuring, the list goes on. For our intubated children there is oral care three times a shift. They are also under constant watch, as children tend to want to pull anything out of their mouths that doesn't belong. I don't blame them. I would too at that age. I still do.

Every day I walk an all too narrow line between life and death, like a sleep-deprived tightrope walker. I can't tell you how many patients I've lost. I don't want to know. It's just part of my job in helping to keep alive as many children as possible.

Once, one of the med school students brought in a medical advice book with the offensive title *Kill as Few People as Possible*. Ironically, it's usually the students, the ones with the least to boast about, who have the biggest egos. He left the book in one of my rooms where a patient or, more likely, one of my patients' parents might see it. It made me so angry that I threw it away. Later, when he came looking for it, I let him have it. In the hierarchy of things, nurses don't tell off doctors—even the students—but if it comes down to massaging a doctor's ego or protecting my patients, there's no question what I'm going to do. I've become a mama bear, and this is my house. No one is going to reprimand or fire me for caring for my patients. If they did I wouldn't want to work there anyway. Besides, I'm good at what I do.

As I was saying, an ICU is always challenging, but a PICU (Pediatric Intensive Care Unit) presents a whole new level of complication. Adult patients are less likely to start ripping out their intubation, IVs, or PICC lines or refuse to take a lifesaving medication, something I have to anticipate with the children I care for.

But working with children also brings a special humanity as well. I can't imagine ever becoming hardened to seeing one of my kids struggle for life or telling a teddy bear not to be scared because everything will be all right. As I said, I don't know how many times I've had to withdraw care—standing with parents as they watch their child die. To hear the sobs and gasps of grief when the screen flatlines, followed by a cacophony of bells and buzzers, is something they can't pay you enough for. I couldn't tell you how many times I've gone into the nurses' lounge and wept, then took a deep breath, washed my face, and resumed my rounds, because no matter what just happened, someone still needs me. It's one of the most challenging of all the units, the most painful, and, for precisely that reason, the most rewarding. I suppose that's why I've stayed so long.

> *There's this guy at work—he's actually named "Guy"—who has a thing for me. He's a bit of a stalker, albeit a benign one—after three months, he still hasn't gotten up the courage to ask me out. I'm prepared to let him down as gently as possible. My father once told me that guys are called "guys" because of Guy Fawkes, the seventeenth-century terrorist who tried to blow up the Palace of Westminster. I just wish he would find someone else to terrorize.*
> *—Richelle Bach's diary*

A little after lunch I had just completed a set of rounds when I heard someone call my name.

"Hey, Richelle."

I knew the voice before I looked up from my screen. It was

Guy, a pharm tech from the hospital's in-patient pharmacy. I always thought his name fit him. He was lanky and awkward, in personality as well as physique. He was also exasperating—one of those hapless souls who tries too hard to be liked. He was slightly younger than me, late twenties I guessed. His last name was Snell. He'd say, "Last name Snell, like the gastropod but not spelled the same." That kind of explains him too.

He considered himself funny. I suppose he was, just not the way he thought. He told jokes and, when no one laughed, explained the punch line. Sometimes, when he launched into one of his jokes, you didn't know if you should politely listen or put a pencil in your ear, both being equally painful.

When I asked him why he decided to be a tech, he said, "Chippendales wasn't hiring." When I didn't laugh he said, "You know what the Chippendales are? In Las Vegas. They're male dancers."

I exhaled. "I know who they are, Guy."

Inconveniently, Guy had a thing for me. It was painfully obvious, not just to me but to everyone in our unit. The first time I met Guy he was standing in front of me at the hospital café checkout counter. He was short a dollar and was telling the woman at the register a convoluted story about why he didn't have enough money on him. I'm not sure what he was trying to accomplish, since I was pretty sure the woman didn't have the authority or inclination to give him anything free, but my lunch breaks are short enough, so finally I just handed him a dollar to speed things up. *A buck*, I thought. *It's worth it.* Had I known the real cost, I wouldn't have thought that.

He immediately introduced himself ("Last name Snell, like

the gastropod . . ."), then thanked me so profusely you'd have thought I'd given him a kidney instead of a dollar. It was sort of like when you give a stray dog some food and then it hangs around your house for the next month. In his case, much longer. I don't mean to be mean, it's just how it was. Or he was. I wondered if I was the only woman who had ever been nice to him—which, the more I got to know him, the more likely it seemed. People hungry for attention are like that, always sniffing for scraps of acceptance.

From then on, Guy came every day to deliver our patients' prescriptions and, in his words, "check up on me." He could have just used the hospital pneumatic delivery system, which is what the internal pharmacists usually did, but that wouldn't give him an excuse to see me.

The others in my unit called him my groupie, as in, "Richelle, your groupie dropped by today," "Richelle, your groupie was asking about you," "Richelle, your groupie says he'll be back later."

Only this time he found me. Another day, another Guy.

"Good afternoon, Guy," I said. "What's up?"

"The sky," he said. "I'm on break."

I gave a slight groan. "And again you decided to spend it in the PICU?"

"Well, I was thinking of traveling to Nepal, but I couldn't get a flight out on that short notice."

"Well, then, it's probably for the best."

"So, what's new with you?"

I continued looking over my charts. "Not much since yesterday afternoon."

"So, this morning one of the patients told me her doctor said she should walk every day. She asked me what I thought of that. I said, 'Ten years ago my grandmother started walking five miles every day. We have no idea where she is.'"

"Yeah, I've heard that one."

"Here's one I bet you haven't heard. Yesterday one of the nurses on six gave a prescription for Losartan to an eighty-eight-year-old woman. Then last night the woman asked her doctor why he'd prescribed her birth control pills."

"Losartan?"

"Right, blood pressure medicine. Anyhoo, her doctor asked, 'Who told you those were birth control pills?'

"She told him, 'The nurse.'

"So the doctor asked the nurse why she'd told his patient they were birth control pills. At first, she couldn't figure out why the woman would say that. Then she remembered she'd told her that the pills were in a child-resistant container."

I laughed, which pleased Guy immensely.

"True story." He leaned against the wall. ". . . And we have no idea where she is . . . Bada boom." He flipped his wrists like he was playing the drums. "Just when you think people can't be any more stupid."

"She's eighty-eight," I said. "Give her some grace."

"Yeah, I should." He sighed lightly, then said, "Speaking of grace, I was wondering if you have plans next Tuesday."

*Tortured segue. Was he actually going to finally ask me out?*

"I'm working. What's up?"

"I mean, after work. Around seven thirty."

"Tuesday night I have my writers group."

"You're a writer?"

"I'm trying to be."

"Well, J. K. Rowling, if you can put your pen aside for an evening, I have two lower arena tickets to Imagine Dragons."

"I'm sorry, but I can't miss this Tuesday. I'm leading the discussion."

He just looked at me blankly. The silence fell into the realm of awkwardness.

"What are Imagine Dragons?" I asked.

His eyebrows rose almost comically. "You're kidding me, right? *Imagine Dragons.*" He said the words louder and slower the way some Americans do when they're trying to communicate with someone who doesn't speak English. ". . . One of the greatest bands of this century."

"That's a low bar."

"I don't think you're getting this. I scored tickets to one of the hottest concerts of the year."

"Congratulations. I'm sorry I don't know who they are. I'm just not much into the modern rock scene."

"What kind of music are you into?"

"Classical. Mostly. Some oldies. Give me a symphony. Or the Stones."

"You mean that boring old stuff?"

"You think Stravinsky and Jagger are boring?"

He didn't answer.

"I read somewhere that people of above-average intelligence are more likely to prefer classical instrumental music than . . . less intelligent people."

His brow furrowed. "Are you saying I'm less intelligent?"

"I'm saying that I like classical music." I stopped what I was doing and looked up at him. "Are you trying to sell me your tickets or are you asking me out?"

He leaned toward me. I could smell corn chips on his breath. "Do you want to be asked out?"

The question was a land mine. Last February I'd turned down another employee's advances, and he'd made my life miserable until he transferred to another unit.

"I'm sorry, but I have a personal policy that I don't date people at work. It creates too many problems."

"So, if one of the doctors asked you out . . ."

"I'd say no."

"How about a cardiologist?"

"Especially a cardiologist."

"They're loaded."

"With ego," I said. "I need to get back to work before one of them yells at me."

Guy sighed demonstratively. "All right, I'll give you until tomorrow to think about it." Then he added, "I'm sure I won't have trouble finding someone who wants to go. Imagine Dragons. You know, going, going, gone."

"I'm sure you won't," I said. "Have a good time."

He looked frustrated that his threat hadn't worked the way he'd hoped. "All right."

A minute later Amelia, one of my coworkers, walked up to me. Amelia had started on the unit about a year earlier. She was petite, maybe five foot one, with short, auburn hair. What she lacked in height she made up in attitude. She seemed to have an opinion on just about everything, especially men, and was never afraid to share it. Coincidentally, I worked more shifts with her than any other nurse in my unit, and we'd gotten close. She was a good nurse but lately had been struggling with her own health problems. "Thanks for covering my shift Monday. Again."

"No worries. How are your migraines?"

"They come and go. Mostly come."

"My sister used to suffer from migraines. What are you taking for them?"

"Sumatriptan. Oral."

"Is it helping?"

She shrugged. "I can't tell."

"That's kind of an answer, isn't it?"

"I guess. So, did I just hear Guy offer you Imagine Dragons tickets?"

"He offered to take me to the concert."

"And you said no?"

"I don't date coworkers."

"Coworkers or Guy?"

"In his case, both."

"Then you wouldn't mind if I went with him?"

"You want to go out with Guy?"

"No. But I want to go to the concert."

"That's a slippery slope," I said. "But if you're feeling brave, go for it."

"I think I will." She turned to go, then stopped. "Oh, almost forgot. Terri wants to see you. She asked me to come find you."

Terri was our unit manager, a position above the charge

nurse and second only to the director. She was older than me by two decades and had an all-business personality, which is probably why we got along so well. "Am I in trouble?"

"I hope so."

"Thanks."

I walked down the hallway to Terri's office. I knocked on her partially opened door, then pushed it open enough to look inside. Terri was sitting behind a desk shrouded with papers.

"You wanted to see me?"

"Richelle. Come in and shut the door, please."

"That sounds ominous," I said, pulling the door shut behind me. "Am I in trouble?"

"Why is it that people always think they're in trouble when I call them to my office?"

"Probably because you only call people to your office when they're in trouble."

She grinned slightly, which was about as much emotion as she ever showed. "Fair enough. But no, you're not in trouble. Have a seat."

I sat down in the padded chair in front of her desk. "What's up?"

"I was just working on scheduling. As usual, I have myriad requests to get Thanksgiving and Christmas off, requests from just about everyone but you."

"I don't need them off."

"Apparently. You haven't taken any time off, vacation or sick leave, in almost a year. Not to mention you've picked up extra shifts."

"That's because Amelia's been having a lot of migraines lately. Is there a problem with that?"

"Maybe," she said. "I know this is a little unusual, but the reason I wanted to talk to you is more personal than business. You're an excellent employee, Richelle. You're smart, you're hardworking, you're dependable. Frankly, I wish I could have a hundred of you. That's why I'm feeling a little protective. I don't want you to burn out."

"I'm not going to burn out."

"Everyone burns out. It's why our turnover is so high. Combine the stress of the job and the schedule you keep, and it's only a matter of time before it's too much. I've been doing this a long time. No one ever thinks they're burning out until they do. And by then it's too late. I'm also told that you volunteer to take the sickest of the children."

"I want to help them."

"That's great, but it just adds to the stress. Honestly, Richelle, a little time off wouldn't kill you."

"You're asking me to work less?"

"I'm asking you to take better care of yourself. You're an asset to our team. I'd work you twenty-four-seven if I could, but a bent bow eventually loses its spring, you know?" Her expression grew more serious. "In addition to the patients we've lost, you've suffered some big personal losses as well. People need time to grieve."

"I've grieved."

She looked doubtful, but lifted her hands in surrender. "All right. I've said my piece. If you change your mind about taking some time off, let me know. I'll give you right of first refusal."

"Thank you."

"Thank you for being you."

"It's all I know how to be."

I returned to my rounds. Terri was right, of course. I hadn't taken a vacation or sick day since my father died, which was only exacerbated by Michelle's death. I suppose it was how I was coping with loss. Or maybe it was how I was handling my loneliness. Still, as I walked away, a little voice inside my head scolded, "Get a life, woman."

# CHAPTER

## *four*

*Today a new man showed up at our writers group. I know nothing about him other than that he's gorgeous, knows how to wear a leather jacket, and smells a little like myrrh. When I asked him if he'd be coming back, he asked me if I was. When I said yes, he said he would too. He's flirting with me, right? It's been so long since someone I was interested in showed interest in me that I don't trust my instincts anymore. Then again, with my relationship history, my instincts have all the reliability of a GPS without an Internet connection. All I know for sure is that if something, or someone, looks too good to be true, they usually are.*

*—Richelle Bach's diary*

## TUESDAY, NOVEMBER 12

We called ourselves the Calliope Writers Group, named after the muse of eloquence and epic poetry in Greek mythology—admittedly a bit high-handed for the level of writers we were. We were about as eclectic a group of writers as you could imagine—from a purple heart–carrying veteran to a self-appointed shaman.

We met for an hour to ninety minutes every Tuesday and Thursday at the Holladay Library, just a mile from my home. After my father died, I found this group online and had been meeting with them since.

There were usually about a dozen in attendance—seven of us were regulars who rarely missed a meeting. Every one of us was working on a book except for Sara, who didn't have any plans to write a book but liked talking about the writing process. (Or maybe she just liked hanging out with us.) We usually had a couple of lookie-loos who came to check us out, then never came back.

Each of us took turns leading the discussion and so every few months, I was assigned a night to come up with a topic, which we would discuss for the first half of the meeting. The last half of our gathering was devoted to sharing our writing to a captive audience.

Tuesday night really was my turn to lead the discussion (I hadn't just made that up for Guy), so I went directly from the hospital to the library to prepare. The topic I had chosen for discussion was "Is anything off-limits for a writer?"

It had started snowing around noon and I worried that the weather would discourage attendance, something, I admit, I really only cared about when I was in charge.

When I arrived, the library was unusually quiet. I had with me my coffee (it was against library rules for patrons to bring drinks into the library, but I'd been coming for so long that the staff just looked the other way), some handouts I'd made copies of at work, a few books on writing, and the binder that held the manuscripts I was working on. I always brought my manuscripts even though I rarely shared from them.

We were such regulars that the library director had given us our own key to the small conference room, which we handed off at the end of each meeting to the next discussion leader.

The room was set up theater style, with three rows of chairs in a half circle facing a whiteboard and a screen that dropped from the ceiling, which I thought was nice to have even though none of us had ever used it.

I wrote down the night's discussion topic on the whiteboard then sat down on a chair at the front of the room to await our members.

The first to arrive was Fred, a former Navy SEAL who was working on a novel about espionage and conspiracy and, in his words, "love that will not be denied." He had lost a leg in the Iraq War, though with his prosthetic leg you wouldn't know unless he told you, which he eventually would. One time, to emphasize a point, he stabbed a knife into his false leg, which, not surprisingly, evoked a gasp from the newbies in the group. Fred loved the shock value.

By five minutes before seven most of our group had drifted in. Surprisingly, there were a few more attendees than usual, almost twenty. We had two people I didn't recognize and a few we hadn't seen in a while. Most surprising was Becky, a tall, bespeckled thirtysomething brunette. She had left the group three months earlier in a fit when Fred had criticized something she was writing.

I was about to begin the discussion when someone else new

walked into the room. He was tall, a little over six feet, with tousled mocha-brown hair that matched his thick brows and deep-set eyes. He wore a leather jacket with a knit wool scarf draped around his neck. In one hand he held a water bottle, in the other a small notebook. My first thought was that he looked gorgeous. He also looked a little lost, as if he wasn't sure if he was in the right place.

"Hi," I said. He turned toward me, then froze. For a moment he just stared at me long enough that I felt awkward. Everyone turned back to see who I was speaking to. "Are you in the right place?"

The question seemed to break him from his trance. "Sorry, yes. I think so. This is the meeting for the homebrewers association?"

Everyone laughed.

"No, this is—"

He raised a hand, grinning. "I'm just kidding. This is a writers group, right?"

"You're in the right place," I said. "Take a seat."

"Thank you." He walked down and sat in the front row, his dark brown eyes set on me the whole way.

As usual, we started our meeting by having the new attendees introduce themselves. First was a stylishly dressed young blond woman.

"Hi, I'm Abigail," she said brightly. "You can call me Abby. I'm technically not a newbie since I came here last fall, but then school got a little too busy. I'm Charlene's friend. I'm writing scary fantasy. Goblins and lycans."

"Hi, Abby," welcomed the chorus. I always wanted to laugh when they did that. I thought we sounded like an AA meeting.

The next newcomer was a short, bald man with a protruding belly. He wore a T-shirt that said *Obey My Dog*.

"Sir, if you'll introduce yourself."

He stood awkwardly, adjusting his oversized glasses and looking around the room cautiously, as if he were about to make a gymnastic dismount. "I'm Gary."

"Hi, Gary," replied the chorus.

"Where are you from, Gary?" I asked.

"I'm from Brigham City. I'm working on a book that proves the earth is flat."

"Then you're writing fiction," Fred said.

More laughter.

Gary didn't see the humor. "No, sir. It's nonfiction. It's well researched."

"Brigham City," I said quickly, steering the conversation away from disaster. "You drove a long way to be here."

"You could have fallen off the edge of the earth," Fred murmured.

I ignored him. "How did you find out about us?"

"My sister works for the Salt Lake library system. She's over at the Whitmore Library."

"Thank you, Gary. Please tell your sister that the library system has been good to us."

I looked over at the other newcomer, the man who had entered last. "Sir?"

He pointed to himself. "Me?"

I nodded. "Please."

He stood, scratching his head as he rose. "Thank you." He looked around the room. I noticed Marjorie heavily eyeing him. Marjorie was one of the regulars. She was trying to break into the romance genre and looked the part. She was pretty in a Barbie sort of way. Blond, perfectly coiffed hair and bright blue eyes beneath thick butterfly lashes. She had once had a gig as a Marilyn Monroe impersonator. The first thing she wrote was a self-help booklet called *Awakening Your Inner Marilyn.* When new guys came they were always interested in her. I figured this would be a rerun.

"You can call me J.T.," he said.

"Hi, J.T.," came the welcome.

He looked as amused by the welcome as I was.

"Thank you for that. This is my first time here. I'm sure you know that. That's pretty much it."

"That was succinct," I said. "You have a good name for an author."

"Thank you. I've heard that."

"A good face too," Marjorie said, then added, "I mean, for the jacket cover."

*Coquette,* I thought.

The man grinned slightly. "Thank you," he said again, then sat down.

He was still looking at me when I looked away from him. "My name is Richelle Bach, like the composer. Tonight's topic is, as I've written on the board, 'Is anything off-limits for a writer?' So, let's open it up to discussion. What do you think?"

"Define what you mean by 'off-limits,' " Charlene blurted out. Charlene was always the first to speak, usually with nothing helpful to say.

"Off-limits as in *off*-limits," I said. "Forbidden, prohibited, banned . . ."

*"Verboten,"* Fred offered. Fred was also a regular and the most outspoken member of our group, as Becky would attest. "This is a timely subject. Western civilization was founded on the ideal of free expression. Freedom of the press and speech were things people would die for. Now they don't mean anything. If you say something someone doesn't agree with, they label it hate speech and call on the social media mob to censor you. It's a slippery slope."

"Thank you, Fred. Who else has a thought on this?"

Becky raised her hand. "I think as writers we need to be sensitive to other people's feelings. We shouldn't write anything that might hurt someone's feelings."

"I think that's true for personal interactions on social media," Marjorie said. "But not books."

"What's the difference?" Becky said. "Media's media."

" *'Feelings,'* " Fred sang disparagingly. " 'Nothing more than *feelings.'* "

Everyone laughed.

"Worst song ever," Marjorie said.

"You see," Fred said, "that's exactly what I'm talking about. I'm pretty sure that the Declaration of Independence hurt King George's feelings."

"That wasn't very sensitive," Becky replied.

Tamara, a recently divorced mother with two autistic sons, spoke next. "The problem is, sometimes the truth is offensive. That doesn't mean it shouldn't be shared. People who once complained about censorship are now the ones promoting it, under the guise of cultural sensitivity. The next thing you know they'll be censoring Dr. Seuss."

"She's right," Fred said.

"You're overreacting," Becky said.

"Am I?" Fred said.

Becky pushed her glasses farther up her nose, something she did when she was upset. "No one's going to censor Dr. Seuss."

Sophia, the lone black woman in our group, said, "Frankly, I'm a little tired of white people telling me what I should be offended by. I think I can figure it out. In fact, I think that's a kind of racism itself. To me, it says I'm weak or stupid, and you know I'm not either of those."

"Well spoken," Fred said. *"Bravo."*

*"Brava,"* Sophia said. "I'm a woman."

"I don't get it," Fred said.

Tamara looked at me. "Richelle, you're ethnic, what do you think?"

Before I could speak, Fred said, "Look, what it all comes down to is, do we want a *nice* society or a free one? Because I guarantee, once it's not free, it's not going to be nice. And the idiots claiming to be kind are anything but."

Abby timidly raised her hand. "Not to completely change the subject, but I have a different kind of question."

"Let's hear it," I said.

"What if you're writing a true story, like about abuse you suffered as a child, but the people you're writing about are still alive. Do you have to change the names? Is it okay to write about other people?"

"If we couldn't write about other people, then there would be nothing written," Sophia said. "There would be no newspapers or blogs."

*"Brava,"* Fred said. "I was raised with the idea that I might not like what you say but I'll defend to the death your right to say it. What happened to that? These brain-dead millennials have no idea that their social media lynch mobs are more evil than the people they attack."

Deborah, a regular who had written three self-published novels, said, "I have a more pragmatic take on it. Writing is hard enough. Having someone else in your head all the time makes it almost impossible to write anything worth reading. Sylvia Plath said, 'Everything in life is writable about if you have the outgoing guts to do it, and the imagination to improvise.' I think one of the worst enemies of creativity is self-doubt. So I say everything is fair game. Creativity demands it. If someone thinks it's offensive, they don't have to read it."

"Who is Sylvia Plath?" Becky asked.

"You know, *The Bell Jar?"*

"Never heard of it."

"It's a classic of feminist thought," Sophia said.

"All right," I said, taking back the reins. "Here's something to think about. I've printed a list of books that have been deemed offensive. I made extra copies, but right now I'll just read it." I looked down at my paper. *"The Catcher in the Rye* by J. D. Salinger. *The Great Gatsby* by F. Scott Fitzgerald. *To Kill a Mockingbird* by Harper Lee. *The Color Purple* by Alice Walker. *The Lord of the Flies* by William Golding. *1984* and *Animal Farm* by George Orwell. *Of Mice and Men* and *The Grapes of Wrath* by John Steinbeck. *Brave New World* by Aldous Huxley. *The Sun Also Rises* and *For Whom the Bell Tolls* by Ernest Hemingway. *As I Lay Dying* by William Faulkner. *The Call of the Wild* by Jack London. *Gone with the Wind* by Margaret Mitchell. . . ." I put down my paper. "The list goes on and on. What do you think? Should these books not exist?"

"Some of them shouldn't . . ." Becky said.

Her response exploded into heated argument. Throughout it all, the new guy, J.T., just calmly sat there, looking amused. After what seemed a long enough time, I looked down at my watch, then said, "Okay, that's enough for now." I turned to J.T. "You've been quiet through all this. Do you have any thoughts on the matter?"

He smiled broadly, then said, "It's just my opinion, but I've read that the best writers write for themselves, so to constantly worry about what others are going to think is going to handicap you, like this woman said." He looked at Deborah.

"I'm Deborah," Deborah said, smiling at having been singled out by him.

"Nice to meet you, Deborah." J.T. turned back to me. "Imagine if you told Van Gogh to limit his palette, or Picasso to paint what was socially correct, we wouldn't have the art we have today. Expression requires freedom. It seems to me that no matter what you say in this world, someone will be offended.

"Also, in response to what Abby asked, I think your story is your story. You own it. If someone doesn't like what's being said about them, then maybe they should have behaved better."

Everyone laughed.

"There you have it," I said. "Kindness and freedom can co-exist. Thank you, J.T." I looked back over the group. "We've already gone over our time and with the weather like it is, we won't be sharing tonight, unless some of you want to stick around and do it on your own time. We have the room for another half hour. For those new here tonight, if you didn't sign in when you came in, please do so before you leave. Our next meeting is this Thursday." I held out the library keys, which were attached to a large stress-ball keychain in the shape of a globe. "Marshall, I bestow the keys to the kingdom."

Marshall stood up and I tossed them to him, badly, almost hitting Marjorie in the head.

"We'd love for you all to join us," I said. Subconsciously, perhaps, as I said this I looked over at J.T. "We hope to see you all here."

J.T. just smiled at me. I took a breath. "I'll end with a quote from Anton Chekhov. 'Don't tell me the moon is shining; show me the glint of light on broken glass.' Good night, everyone."

After the meeting, J.T. just sat while everyone else gathered their things. I walked over to him. "Well, newcomer, what did you think?"

"Why was the glass broken?"

"The glass?"

"The quote you shared."

"I don't know. I suppose that's the point of good writing, to make you curious. But what I was asking was, what did you think of our discussion tonight?"

"I enjoyed it. Are you this group's president?"

"No. We don't have a president. We don't even have a leader. We take turns leading the discussions."

"Well, you did a good job of riling everyone up. For a moment I thought a brawl might break out. Is it always this lively?"

"No. Usually we have to check pulses to see if they're still alive. Are you coming to the next meeting?"

He looked at me for a moment then asked, "Are you?"

"I'm planning on it."

He nodded. "Then I will."

"Good. Then I'll see you here."

He stood there a moment, his eyes set on mine, and then, with surprising intensity, he said, "It's really nice meeting you, Richelle. Have a good night."

As he walked out of the room, Marjorie scurried out after him. I hoped he really did come back on Thursday. I wanted to get to know him better.

# CHAPTER

*five*

*I think Guy took one of my coworkers to the concert just to make me jealous. Or maybe she was the only one he could find who would go out with him. Either way, I'm good with it. I told him that I wasn't interested in the music, but the truth is, with the right guy (no pun intended), I'd be content listening to grass grow.*

—*Richelle Bach's diary*

## WEDNESDAY, NOVEMBER 13

The next morning, Amelia and I walked into work together. She looked tired, as if she'd stayed up too late.

"So did you go to the concert with Guy?"

"I did."

"How was it?"

"It was a great concert."

"How was Guy?"

"It was a great concert."

"I figured as much. Did he ask you out again?"

"Of course."

"I warned you," I said. "Slippery slope."

An hour or so later Guy came down for his usual visit. I was at the nurses' station filling out reports.

"You missed an amazing concert last night," he said, leaning against the counter.

"No doubt. I heard it was great."

"It. Was. Incredible." He nodded slowly. "I took someone from the hospital." I think he was trying to make me jealous.

"Amelia?" I said.

His smile fell. "Did she tell you?"

"Lucky guess," I said. "So, are you going out again?"

He tried to act cool. "Well, she wants to, but we'll see. I'm kind of busy. I've got a side hustle I've been working on. It's going to make millions. It's an app."

"Good luck with that," I said.

"Yeah, I'd tell you more about it, but best I keep it under wraps for now. NDAs and all that. That means non-disclosure agreements."

"Probably a good idea you keep it on the down-low. You don't want someone to steal your idea."

"Exactly." His head bobbed like one of those dolls. "Well, I better get back. We're a little slammed today."

"Bye."

He was about to leave when he stopped. "You know, if you're dying to know what I'm working on, maybe we could get a coffee sometime. Is that against your policy?"

"I better ask Amelia. I wouldn't want her to think I was trying to move in . . ."

"Oh, we're just friends," he said quickly.

"I'll think about it," I said. "Have a good day."

# CHAPTER

*six*

*Tonight, our writers' discussion was on how long a book should be.*
*I don't think anyone could give better advice on the matter than*
*Lewis Carroll: "Begin at the beginning . . . and go on till you come*
*to the end: then stop." The best part of the evening came after the*
*meeting when J.T. asked me out to dinner. They say you don't know*
*the book until you open its cover, but open or not, I still feel like I'm*
*reading a mystery.*

—*Richelle Bach's diary*

## THURSDAY, NOVEMBER 14

I arrived at the writers group about ten minutes early, hoping to talk to J.T. before the discussion began, but to my disappointment he wasn't there. Instead, I ended up talking to Marshall, who was leading the night's discussion. Marshall was, at least financially, the most successful of the group. He owned a downtown office supply company, which I figured was doing well, since I had seen him in television commercials and he drove a lemon-yellow Maserati.

He was always well dressed, usually in a sport jacket over a loud Italian Bugatti shirt. I knew the brand only because James swore by them.

Marshall was one of our group's nonfiction writers and a motivational speaker, though just for his company's clients so far. He had written several books and self-published them, selling them at his store and the back of the room at his speaking events.

His first two books, *The Marshall Way* and *Marshall Law*, had basically flopped, selling less than a hundred copies in total. But his third book, *The Five Habits of Smart Business Owners*, was doing much better, and had already sold nearly a thousand copies.

The topic he'd written on the whiteboard for this evening's discussion was "How long should a book be?"

At seven, J.T. still hadn't arrived. I felt surprisingly disappointed. I don't know why. Outside of our brief encounter I didn't even know him. Maybe that's why I was disappointed.

Marshall began the discussion as he usually did, emulating a late-night talk show host giving a monologue.

"Hey, welcome, everyone. Before we begin, I have a question for you. How many motivational speakers does it take to change a light bulb?"

"How many?" someone asked.

"None," he said, pointing at the man, "because the change starts with you."

Even I laughed.

"Last year I threw a boomerang. Now I live in constant fear.

"What did the duck say when she bought lipstick? Just put it on my bill."

"For the love of Pete, please stop already," Fred said.

Marshall smiled. "I have one for you, army man. The general said to the sergeant, 'How many soldiers you got?' He said, 'Nineteen, sir!' 'All right, Sergeant, round them up.' 'Okay, twenty, sir.' "

Fred just shook his head. "I give up."

"A good soldier never gives up," Marshall said. "But I digress. Let's begin. You can read the board; the million-dollar question tonight is, 'How long should a book be?' "

"That depends on the genre," Charlene said, in a surprisingly helpful comment. "Sci-fi and fantasy books need to be longer because of all the world-building that takes place." She referenced *Lord of the Rings* and *Hunger Games* and, of course, her own book, *The Alien Gene*.

As usual, Fred was generous with his opinions. "A book's length," he said, "should be like a woman's dress—long enough to cover the essentials but short enough to keep it interesting."

Everyone laughed except Marjorie who, I noticed, was wearing an unusually short skirt, no doubt in anticipation of seeing J.T.

"That's sexist," she said.

"Sue me," Fred replied.

I was about to add my thoughts to the discussion when I noticed Marjorie's head whip to the door. I turned to see J.T. walking in. He was wearing the same leather jacket as last time, but now it was open, revealing an unbuttoned long sleeve collared shirt over a black tee. He was even more handsome than I had remembered him. Marjorie waved him over. He smiled, mouthed a thank-you, then, to my surprise, pointed toward me as if we'd made some previous arrangement to sit together.

Marjorie's gaze followed him as he walked over to my side of the room. He gestured to the chair next to mine. "Mind if I sit here?"

I tried not to act too pleased. "Not at all."

"Thank you." He took off his coat, folded it in half, and draped it across the chair next to him then sat down. "Sorry I'm late."

Marshall, who had noticed the distraction caused by J.T.'s entrance, said, "Welcome, fellow writer. Are you new here?"

"No, I was here the other night. I'm J.T."

"Hello, J.T.," the group echoed. Seriously, it was Pavlovian.

"Sorry I'm late," he said. "There was an accident on Highland Drive."

"I saw that," Marjorie said. "Are you okay?"

J.T. looked at her. "I wasn't in the accident. I was just trying to get by it."

"Oh. Good," she said, acting relieved.

"No worries," Marshall said. "We've been discussing how long a book should be. Do you have any thoughts on the subject?"

"How long a book should be?" he repeated. "I guess that depends on the book."

"You mean the genre?"

"No, I mean if it's any good. There are books I never

wanted to end. And I've read a few books that I wish had ended after the first page."

Marshall laughed. "Well said." He looked back out at everyone else. "So, how long for a young adult book?"

J.T. leaned over to me. "How was your day?"

"Good. How was yours?"

"Not bad."

I said something uncharacteristically forward. "I was afraid you weren't coming. I'm glad you're here."

He smiled. "Thank you. Me too."

In spite of Fred's best efforts, the discussion lacked controversy, so it didn't go on nearly as long as mine had. Marshall read a chapter from the new book he was working on, *The Marshall Plan* (an awful title, I thought), then opened the meeting up to the group to share their writing.

"Are you going to read from your book?" J.T. asked.

I shook my head. "No. I'm not ready to share it yet. How about you?"

He lifted his hands. "I've got nothing."

It was just a down night. Even Fred, who always had something to share, remained silent. Marshall dismissed the meeting early. I noticed Marjorie give J.T. a furtive glance then hurry out. As the others started to leave, J.T. turned to me. "I know it's late, but would you like to get a cup of coffee or maybe something to eat? I didn't have dinner tonight."

"That sounds nice. I didn't have time for dinner either."

"I passed an Italian restaurant on the way here. Just off 6200 South."

"Tuscany," I said. "But, it's kind of formal."

"Does that mean we'll need reservations?"

"No. I just meant it's the kind of place you go to on a special occasion."

"Going to dinner with you would be a special occasion."

I smiled. "That was nice."

"I'm glad you thought so. Would you like to drive together or should I meet you there?"

"I can meet you there."

"Then we should share phone numbers, in case one of us gets lost."

I figured it was a ruse to get my phone number, not that I minded sharing it. "One of *us*?"

"By 'us' I mean me," he said.

"All right, I'll send you my number. What's yours?"

"938-555-6219."

I typed it in, then looked up. "Where is the 938 area code?"

"Huntsville, Alabama. I've had my phone awhile."

"All right, Huntsville." I sent him my contact information.

He helped me on with my coat, then we walked out the library's front doors into the brisk winter air. We passed some of the group members who had gathered outside to talk, then walked to the parking lot. J.T. was parked just a few cars from me. I noticed that he was driving a car with an Oklahoma license plate. *Alabama. Oklahoma. Utah. Whoever he was, he got around.* I pulled out of the library's parking lot with J.T. trailing close behind me.

Tuscany is a cozy cottage-like restaurant located in the wooded foothills of the Wasatch Mountains. It was opened by former Utah Jazz basketball player Mark Eaton, and the restaurant's signature dessert, the 7′ 4″ chocolate cake, was created in homage to him.

The restaurant was only a few miles from the library. I parked my car, then waited outside the restaurant's massive metal-trimmed front door for J.T., who had gotten stuck at a traffic light. A moment later he pulled in. He parked his car and ran up to meet me.

We walked inside the restaurant's beautiful stone-tile entry, which was already decorated for the holidays. Garlands and glass baubles hung from the ceiling, and in the corner of the room was a twelve-foot Christmas tree elaborately decorated with strands of golden lights, silk ribbons, and blown-glass ornaments.

The walls were a dark cream stucco adorned with golden-framed oil landscapes of the Tuscan countryside. Across the entryway from us, a young woman dressed in all black stood behind a hostess table. She smiled at us as we entered.

"Welcome to Tuscany. Do you have a reservation?"

"We don't," J.T. said, stepping up to the table. "It was kind of a last-minute decision. Can we still get in?"

"Absolutely."

"We'd like someplace private, if possible."

She grabbed a couple of menus. "I can put you in the Mural Room. You'll be the only guests."

"Thank you."

The hostess led us upstairs along a circular stairwell. The room was small, with only four tables and three walls, which were painted with frescoes depicting Italian hillsides and farmlands. The room overlooked a blown-glass chandelier that resembled a Chihuly.

"How is this?" the hostess asked.

J.T. deferred to me. "Is this okay?"

"It's nice, thank you."

"It's perfect," J.T. said.

J.T pulled out my chair then sat down across from me as the hostess lit the candle in the middle of the table.

*"Buon appetito,"* she said. "Your waitress will be right with you." J.T. immediately straightened his napkin and silverware. I was happy to see that he had OCD like me.

"This is even fancier than I remember," I said.

"Maybe it's the Christmas decorations."

I looked down at the menu. ". . . And a bit more pricey."

"I've got this," he said. "So tell me about yourself."

"What do you want to know?"

"To start, what do you do, other than write books?"

"Work, mostly. Usually."

"What do you do?"

"I'm a nurse in a PICU."

"What's a PICU?"

"It stands for Pediatric Intensive Care Unit. It's an ICU for children."

"That sounds intense."

"Very."

"How often do you work?"

"Always. At least it feels like that. I work from seven to seven three days a week, but lately I've been taking on a lot of extra shifts."

"Do you like it?"

"I do. It takes a unique personality to work there. I think most of the people on our unit are adrenaline junkies. We're a trauma one unit, which means we take the most difficult patients. My kids are usually trying to die on me, and I do everything I can to stop that from happening."

"That's heroic. You're saving lives."

"We try," I said. "Not always. Two days ago I had to withdraw care from a twelve-day-old baby."

"What does that mean, to withdraw care?"

"It means there's nothing more we can do to keep them alive. I had to carry her little body to the morgue."

J.T. frowned. "Did you see the baby's parents?"

"I was with her parents when she passed. It was heartbreaking. No parent should have to bury a child. I don't think I'll ever get used to it." I looked at him. "I hope I never get used to it."

"I would think not."

Neither of us spoke for a moment. Then I said, "Sometimes the parents make the job . . . interesting."

"By *interesting* do you mean fun or a nightmare?"

I grinned. "Both. But when it's bad, it's bad. You wouldn't believe what we have to put up with."

"Tell me about it."

"Well, like yesterday. I had a parent insist that her child needed a prescription for oxycontin for pain. When I told her that her child wasn't in pain, she started screaming at me. She said I was an awful, unfeeling human who obviously didn't care about her child and she wanted to complain to my supervisor. My charge nurse had already heard what was going on. Of course the woman was only trying to get the drug for herself."

"Of course she was."

"You'd be surprised how many addicts are out there."

"No, I wouldn't. My brother works for the DEA."

"Your brother works in drug enforcement?"

He nodded. "He's fairly high up. He's in charge of the DEA's Dallas field office. He's told me some wild stories. People will do anything to get their drugs."

"We have our share of them. A few years ago we had a man come into the ER demanding pseudoephedrine. When the nurse didn't give it to him, he went out to his car and came back with a machete."

"Was anyone hurt?"

"One of the nurses was hurt pretty bad. Fortunately, she was in the ER, so she received immediate attention."

"What happened to the machete guy?"

"He was killed when he went after security."

"What a world we live in," J.T. said. "So, intriguing question: After they shot him, did they try to save him?"

"Of course we did."

He nodded. "Of course you did. What's pseudoephedrine?"

"It's a decongestant. Sudafed."

"Can't you just buy it over the counter?"

"You used to be able to. Then it was taken off the shelves because it can be used to make methamphetamine."

"Crystal meth."

"Right. So now there's a government registry for it."

"The War on Drugs *is* a war. My brother has been in gunfights. He was shot once in the chest. Fortunately, he had his vest on, so it just broke a couple of ribs. I shouldn't say 'just.' He was in a lot of pain for a while, but it's better than dead. The cartels move a lot of drugs through Texas."

"It seems to be getting worse," I said. "Especially the opioids. I once caught a patient stealing a doctor's prescription pad."

"Do the doctors or nurses ever steal drugs?"

"It happens. In nursing school they told us that at least ten percent of medical professionals misuse drugs. Just before I started, there was a nurse on our unit who was caught substituting acetaminophen for oxycontin and giving it to the patients, keeping the opioid for herself. They caught her because all her patients were in pain. It's called drug diversion." I suddenly smiled. "This went dark fast."

"We definitely went down a rabbit hole," he said. "What else should we talk about?"

"How about you?" I asked.

"What would you like to know?"

"What does J.T. stand for? Or is J.T. your full name?"

"The J stands for Justin."

I was glad it wasn't James. "Justin. I like that. And the T?"

"The T stands for my parents' sense of humor."

I cocked my head. "Yes?"

"It stands for True, as in Justin True. You can see why I go by J.T."

"It could be worse."

"How could it be worse?"

"Your middle name could have been Case."

He thought that through, then smiled. "You're right, that would be worse. Seriously, I've kept my middle name under wraps my entire life. You're like one of six people, besides my family, who knows it now."

"How vulnerable of you to share it with me."

"Our relationship just took a huge leap forward," he said. "So, now that you know, you can call me Justin."

"Justin," I said. "I can do that. What's your last name?"

"Ek. E-K. Sounds like you're choking when you say it. It's Swedish."

"Justin Ek."

A waitress walked up to our table. "Hi, I'm sorry I took so long. How are you two tonight?"

"We're fine, thank you," I said.

"Can I get you something to drink?"

"I'll just have water," I said.

"Sparkling or still?"

"Just tap water."

She turned to Justin. "What would you like to drink, sir?"

"Do you have eggnog?"

"Eggnog? I don't think so."

"Then I'll just have water too."

"Very well. I'll be back in a moment to take your order."

After she left, I said, "Eggnog?"

"I like eggnog. It's the season, right?"

"I've just never heard anyone actually order it."

"We're a special breed, we noggers."

"I think you just made that word up."

"I'm absolutely sure I did."

"Did you know there's such a thing as phobia of eggnog? It's called nogophobia."

"I think you just made that up too."

"No, it's real. My dad used to tell my sister and me random facts. It's my curse that I can't forget them."

"Like what?"

"Like the fear of clowns is called coulrophobia."

"Clowns *are* terrifying," he said. "We have John Wayne Gacy and Stephen King to thank for that."

"Then there's nomophobia. That's a relatively new one. It's the fear of being without a smartphone."

"So there's a name for that," he said. "I'm not alone."

"And there's neophobia, the fear of new things."

"I'm impressed that you remembered all those."

"Like I said, it's a curse."

"Speaking of neophobia, you say you've been here before."

I smiled at his segue. "Twice. A few years ago we had a work Christmas party here. And my father brought me once for my birthday."

"In October."

"What are you, psychic?"

He paused for a moment, then said, "No. I just pay attention. It was the opal necklace you're wearing. It's October's birthstone." He lifted his menu. "We probably should decide what we want to eat. What do you recommend?"

"I've had the double-cut pork chop and the puttanesca. Both were really good."

He looked over the menu for a moment, then said, "This late, everything sounds a little heavy; maybe I'll just go with the Tuscan pear salad. How about you?"

"I'll just have the beet salad."

He sighed. "Beets," he said. "I'm willing to bet that there's a fear of beets."

"You don't like beets?"

"When I was a kid, beets were one of those things my mother used for punishment. She once made me sit at the table until I ate all my beets. I sat there for three hours. I'm basically scarred."

"You shouldn't have PTSD over a vegetable."

"And yet I do." He set down his menu. "How many books have you written?"

"If by *written* you mean completed, none. I'm working on two books."

"Tell me about them."

"The first one I started is called *Confessions of a PICU Nurse.*"

"So it's nonfiction?"

"No, it's a novel. But I'm drawing on things that have happened to me in real life at work."

"I love anecdotes. Tell me some."

"Where do I begin? Hospitals are a treasure trove of fodder for drama. That's why there are so many television series based in hospitals. We witness everything from comedy to tragedy."

"Give me some comedy."

"Okay. Last week I was giving a patient some pills. I said,

'You should know that these pills are habit-forming.' She said, 'Rubbish. I've been taking them for nine years.' "

Justin chuckled.

"Another time a woman told me that she was certain her six-year-old daughter had a brain tumor because she was dizzy. After I examined her, I could see that she just had a minor inner ear infection. I told the mother that it wasn't a tumor, she just had vertigo. The mother said 'No, that can't be right. She's a Libra.' "

Justin burst out laughing. "You couldn't make that up."

"I know, right? I've also had some remarkable mystical experiences too. Once I had a little seven-year-old leukemia patient named Mason. One morning I asked him how he was feeling. He said, 'I'm fine, thank you.' Then he told me he would be leaving the hospital soon. I said, 'I don't think you're going anywhere, cowboy. We need you to stay here for a while to get better.' Then he said, 'Yesterday Grandma June told me I was going to go home and be with her.' I said, 'Well, your grandma probably just misses you.'

"When I told his mother what he'd said, she started to cry. Grandma June was the boy's grandmother. She had died three years before he was born, and his mother never talked to him about her. Mason died two days later."

"That's a remarkable story," Justin said.

"And there are the incredible acts of compassion as well. Once we had a five-year-old girl who had been hit by a car. She had lost a lot of blood and needed a massive transfusion. She had a Ro subtype, which we were unusually low on. Her parents told us that her eight-year-old brother also had a Ro subtype, which we could use. I told the little boy that his sister needed his blood and asked if we could take it. He was clearly scared, but he said okay.

"After the girl was stable, I walked out to tell the family that she was okay. The little boy just sat there with tears in his eyes. I said, 'You don't need to worry anymore. Your sister is going to be fine.' He forced a smile, then said, 'How long until I die?' I said, 'What do you mean?' He said, 'I gave her my blood. Doesn't that mean I have to die now?' I reassured him that he wasn't going to die, then I said, 'You thought you were going to die but you still gave your sister your blood?' He said, 'Yes, ma'am.' I asked him why he would do that. He just said, 'She's my little sister.' "

Justin looked moved. "That really happened?"

I nodded. "I had to walk out because I couldn't stop crying."

"It kind of gives you hope for humanity." After a moment he said, "It sounds like a great book. I can't wait to read it."

"Thank you. Maybe someday I'll actually finish it."

"How far along are you?"

"Maybe a third of the way through."

"What's the other book you're working on?"

"It's very different. It's called *The Prodigal Daughter*."

His brow furrowed again. "Tell me about it."

"You can probably guess what it's about from the title."

"I'd guess it's a modern-day retelling of the prodigal son parable except with two sisters."

"That's exactly what it is. Do you know the Bible?"

"Some. I was raised in a religious family. Is this story non-fiction?"

"It's a novel as well. It's about a girl who decides she doesn't want to wait for her father's death to live it up, so instead of going to college she asks her father for her inheritance and runs off to Europe.

"Almost everyone has heard the prodigal son story, but there are a couple things people usually get wrong about it."

"What are they?"

"First, most people think the word *prodigal* means wayward or lost. It doesn't. Prodigal means lavish or wastefully extravagant. It's like spending money recklessly. It also means to give on a lavish scale. So, in the case of the prodigal son story, you could argue that the father was prodigal since he gave his love freely, on a lavish scale. You might even say recklessly."

"That's beautiful," he said. "I've always believed love should be a little reckless. Sometimes a lot."

I liked that he said that.

"What's the other thing people get wrong about the story?"

"The other is that people don't think through the fact that when the son takes his father's inheritance, his father is literally giving away his own life. An inheritance is usually what's left after someone's death. But to take the money before he dies is to take from him."

Justin looked at me more intensely. "You're sure this isn't based on someone?"

"Maybe a little." I was glad he didn't press.

"How about you?" I asked. "What are you working on?"

"I'm still in the soft clay developmental phase."

"What does that mean?"

"It means I haven't started anything and I didn't want you to know that."

"First rule of our writers group is no shame. When you start your book, what genre will you be writing in?"

"I don't know. I'm thinking of writing a spy novel. It's either that or a cookbook."

I laughed. "You can cook?"

"Not really."

"That could be a problem," I said.

He grinned. "I've considered that."

"Well, maybe you could combine the two. A secret agent disguised as a chef who poisons people with his delicious cooking. You could put recipes in the back of your book, but, like, substitute baking soda for cyanide."

"Brilliant. Should I ever actually get around to putting pen to paper, that's what I'll write."

Our conversation paused as our waitress brought a bottle of water to the table, poured our glasses, then took our dinner orders. After she left, I asked, "How did you hear about Calliope?"

"Calliope?"

"You know, the writers group we just came from."

"Oh. Of course. A friend told me about it."

"Was he a member?"

"She. And no. She read about it online."

"I noticed that you have Oklahoma license plates, but you have an Alabama area code."

"You're observant."

"I pay attention too," I said.

"The Oklahoma plates are because I have a rental car. I've only been in Utah for a few weeks. How about you? Where's home?"

"I've lived in Salt Lake all my life, except when I went to the University of Texas for nursing school."

"Why Texas?"

"It was one of the top nursing schools in the country. And they offered me a scholarship. Did you go to school?"

"Caltech."

His answer surprised me a little. "That's impressive. Isn't that hard to get into?"

"It's a bit of a challenge."

"What did you study?"

"Aerospace engineering."

"Aerospace. So that makes you . . ."

"A rocket scientist."

"That's really impressive. What do you do with that?"

"After I graduated, I got a job at the Jet Propulsion Laboratory in Pasadena. I've been there for about eight years."

"So what are you doing in Utah? I can't imagine there's a lot of opportunities here for a rocket scientist."

"More than you think. There are some pretty big aerospace part manufacturers."

Our waitress arrived with our salads. "Can I get you anything else?" she asked.

"No, we're good, thank you," Justin said. After she left, he looked down at his salad. "This looks good." Then he looked at mine. "At least mine does."

"You sure you don't want some of my beets?"

"You're taunting me, aren't you?"

I smiled as I put one in my mouth. A moment later I asked, "You were born in Alabama?"

"Huntsville, Alabama," he said, slipping in a bit of a southern drawl. "Rocket City."

"Hence the career in rockets."

"It definitely gave me a nudge."

"*Rocket* City. That's a good moniker."

"It's a lot better than what it used to be."

"What's that?"

"The watercress capital of the world."

"From watercress to rockets. That's a big leap."

"Astronomical," he said.

I caught the pun but didn't say anything. "You know, I don't think I even know what watercress is."

"It's basically a floating cabbage." He shook his head. "My question is, if you were the watercress capital of the world, would you brag about it?"

"I guess you take your accolades where you can get them."

He smiled. "I suppose we do."

"Back to you," I said. "Do you have any siblings?"

"Three. I have an older brother and sister and a younger sister."

"Are you close?"

"Very. Especially with my brother, Liam. I don't see any of them as much as I'd like, but we talk almost every week."

This was foreign to me, considering that I hadn't talked to my sister for more than six years. "That must be nice. Where do they live?"

"They're scattered around the country. Audra, my older sister, is married with two children. She lives in Columbus, Ohio, with her husband. She's currently a stay-at-home mom, he's an executive for Wendy's. She sends me Wendy's gift cards every month."

"That's a nice perk."

"Yes, I eat a lot of hamburgers and Frostys. My brother lives in Texas. He's not married. Close, but no ring."

"He's the one who works for the DEA?"

"Right. And then there's my younger sister, Kayla. She's pursuing a degree in public relations at Columbia. She did an internship for a major publisher in New York last summer and plans to work for them when she graduates. That connection could come in handy when you finish your books."

"That's good to know. How about your parents? Are they still alive?"

"They're alive and well. My father used to own a large plumbing supply company. He sold it five years ago and retired. Now my parents have never been busier. They live in Texas, but they spend a lot of time traveling. Mostly to Columbus, since that's where their grandchildren are, but they also spend a lot of time in New York. Kayla's there and they love seeing Broadway and off-Broadway shows. That's their thing. A couple years ago they spent a summer in London taking a playwriting course."

"So that's where you got your writing chops?"

"I don't have writing chops. But growing up we were all bookworms. One summer I read sixty-two books. I won an award for that."

"Rub that in my face," I said.

He laughed. "It was the Huntsville Book Nerd award. At that age, I wasn't showing it to anyone."

I said, "My father got mad at me once for spending too much time indoors reading. You and I would have made good friends."

"It's not too late," he said.

That made me smile. "Your family sounds happy."

"Happily boring. It's inconvenient, really. There's no great drama to draw from, so I can't blame all my defects on my parents. Like Tolstoy said, 'All happy families are alike.' "

"And 'each unhappy family is unhappy in its own way,' " I said, finishing the line. "So, with all that familial bliss, why aren't you married?" I regretted the question the second it came out of my mouth.

"I was," he said softly. "She left me." I could see pain in his eyes.

"I'm sorry. I shouldn't have asked."

"It's okay to talk about it."

"Is there a chance of getting back together?"

He shook his head. "No. That won't happen."

"I'm sorry."

He again breathed out heavily. "Yeah, me too."

We were both quiet for a moment. Then I said, "I really shouldn't have asked that."

"No, it's okay. You can ask me anything." He took a drink, then said, "Turnabout is fair play. Why aren't you married?"

"I guess I haven't found the right guy yet."

"And what does the right guy look like?"

"I have no idea."

"Then how will you know when you've found him?"

"I suppose that's a problem."

He nodded thoughtfully. "Tell me about *your* family."

"Not nearly as idyllic as yours. My mother left us when I was three, so I was raised by my father. Which is why my father and I were so close. I have one sister, Michelle. Had. She was my identical twin." I breathed out. "She passed away last June. We were estranged, so I didn't even hear about her funeral until it was over. There were some hard things between us."

He looked thoughtful. "What was that like, being a twin?"

"I'm not sure how to answer that, since it's all I know. Sometimes it was a little complicated. Especially in our case."

"Why in your case?"

"Well, we looked so much alike, but we couldn't have been more different. You know how in biology they talk a lot about scientific twin testing, like twins who were separated at birth and raised thousands of miles apart both play the saxophone, smoke the same brand of cigarettes, and have the same kind of dog. Well, seriously, it wouldn't have worked with us. We were completely different. Maybe not so much when we were young, just later in life."

"Completely different?"

"Pretty much. It's like that prank when they give people caramel apples, only one of them is really an onion. You can't tell which is which until you take a bite."

Justin looked amused by my metaphor. "Which were you? The apple or the onion?"

"Now there's a question," I said. I took a drink of water,

then set my glass down. "I always thought I was the apple. But I'm not so sure anymore."

"Why is that?"

"I don't know. I was always the 'good' one. The pleaser. I obeyed the rules, did my homework. Sometimes I even did Michelle's homework." I shook my head. "Michelle was the rebel. The one who got in trouble. I was in the honor society—she was on the principal's detention list. I was order, she was chaos. I was discipline, she was . . . fun."

"Fun?"

"Yeah, she was fun. At least everyone thought so."

"And you're not?"

"Not especially. I was too uptight. Always worried about things. Worried about her."

"You sound regretful. You think it was a mistake living that way?"

"Obviously, I didn't back then. But now . . . how does the song go, 'your brain gets smart but your head gets dumb.' I sometimes wonder if I was really living my life for everyone else. There's a price to that. I gave up my personal and social life."

"Why did you stop talking to your sister?"

I looked up from my glass. "I'm not ready to talk about that."

"I understand," he said. "Tell me about your father."

I smiled slightly. "I loved my father. He was an interesting man. He was a fighter pilot with the air force. You would never guess it, since he looked more like a mail clerk than a fighter pilot. He flew the A-10."

"The Warthog," Justin said.

I looked at him in amazement. "You know the A-10?"

"The A-10, the Warthog, aka the Tankbuster. Designed for close air support for ground troops. It could fire 3,900 rounds a minute. It could fly with just one engine and one wing. Toughest plane ever built."

"Now I'm impressed. How do you know all this?"

"I told you, I was a book nerd. I wanted to fly when I was young, so I studied every plane ever made, from the Wright Flyer to the SR-71 Blackbird. The A-10 was a unique flying machine. It was aviation's redheaded stepchild."

"My dad used to joke that it was so slow, birds would run into the back of it."

Justin laughed. "No, it wasn't built for speed."

"When my father retired from the air force they gave him an A-10 gun barrel mounted on a plaque. It's still hanging in his bedroom." Talking about my father made me feel sad. "I've never met anyone who knew about the A-10."

"What did your father do after he left the air force?"

"He lived in Taiwan for five years as a private consultant for one of the plane manufacturers. That's where he met my mother. They were married in Taipei, then came to Utah to settle down. He was born here and thought it would be a good place to raise a family."

"He was born in Salt Lake?"

"No, actually he was born in Beaver. It's a small town about two hundred miles south of here. It's hard to believe he came from such a small town but ended up living and working all around the world."

"General John Pershing came from a tiny town in northern Missouri. Walt Disney came from a little town along the same freeway called Marceline. Everyone who became something great had to start from where they were."

"Butch Cassidy came from Beaver, Utah," I said.

"There you go. Infamy." He smiled. "I think your father was a good man."

"Why do you think that?"

"You."

"Thank you," I said softly. "He really was a good man." For a moment I was quiet as melancholy spread through my heart. I took a few bites of my salad, then looked back up at him. "Do you think deathbed promises matter?"

He looked intrigued by the question. "I suppose it depends on whether the promise was rational or not. When you're losing someone, you're emotionally vulnerable. Vulnerable people will say almost anything. Why do you ask?"

"I made my father a promise that I never fulfilled. And now it's too late." Justin didn't ask what the promise was, which I was grateful for. After a moment I looked at him and forced a smile. "It's getting late. I've got work in the morning."

Justin glanced at his watch. "I'm sorry. I forgot we started so late. I better get you home. I'll find our waitress." While I went to the restroom, Justin paid the check. I met him in the restaurant's entry. We snapped a quick picture together, then we walked out to our cars.

"In spite of what you said to the contrary, you are fun," he said. "I had a really nice time. Any chance I could see you again?"

I smiled. "I'd say the odds are pretty good."

"That's good news."

We stopped at my car. I unlocked my door, then looked up at him. "Would you like to come over to my place for dinner?"

"Absolutely I would."

"Are you free this Saturday?"

"I'm sorry, I'm not. I'm leaving town tomorrow. My life's a little mixed up right now, so I have to leave town on the weekends."

"When do you come back?"

"I'll be back Monday afternoon."

"How about dinner Monday evening?"

"Perfect. What time?"

"Seven?"

"I'll be there."

"You'll be where? You don't know where I live."

"Of course," he said. "Maybe you should send me your address."

"I'll text it to you." I took out my phone and shared my contact. When I looked back up he was gazing at me with an unusual intensity.

"I don't mean to be overly forward, but . . . may I kiss you?"

The request surprised me. It's not that I didn't want him to kiss me, I just didn't expect it. "Yes."

He stared deeply into my eyes, then he pulled me in, pressing his lips firmly against mine. It didn't feel like a first kiss. It felt familiar. Satisfying. I didn't want it to end.

Peculiarly, when we parted, he wasn't looking at me. I noticed his eyes were moist. He swallowed, then said softly, "Thank you. I . . ." He stopped. ". . . Tonight was everything I hoped it would be. You really are lovely."

"Thank you, Justin. I'll see you Monday."

He opened my door and I got in. He just stood there as I backed out of the parking spot and drove home.

*Everything he hoped it would be?*

# CHAPTER

*seven*

*I got a new patient today, a fourteen-year-old boy with cancer, purple hair, and an attitude. He was a challenge, but I wonder how challenging I'd be if I were on death row. I asked him what he wanted for Christmas, and he said, "To not die."*

—Richelle Bach's diary

## FRIDAY, NOVEMBER 15

I woke the next morning thinking about Justin. I wish that I had dreamed about him, but I didn't. I dreamt about the opals again. The dream seemed even more intense than usual. At least this time the setting changed. I was standing in the garden behind the Tuscany restaurant.

Neither Michelle nor I ever had trouble attracting men. I had dated since James. Many times. Like Justin, some of the men were gorgeous and successful and kind, but each time, I found a reason to abort the relationship. Something was different about Justin. I don't know how to explain it, but he didn't feel like a stranger. It was as if we'd just skipped over all the awkward parts. Whatever the reason, I wasn't looking for a way to derail things. At least not consciously. I couldn't wait to be with him again.

I rolled into work at the usual hour. Christmas music was playing and the night shift had started decorating the unit for the holidays. There was an unspoken contest as to which shift could come up with the most unique hospital-themed decoration. This had been going on for four years, and had culminated in two large plastic bins of Christmas decorations which sat in the custodial closet for most of the year.

Walking into our unit there was a wreath made from empty pill bottles, which was a huge improvement over the previous one made from urine sample bottles and latex gloves.

Someone had put a new, three-foot-tall Christmas tree on the counter, hung with tiny red LED lights and empty syringes.

Next to it was a perennial, a large glass candy jar with a prescription sign on it that made it look like a medicine jar, even though it was filled with gummy bears. A few years back, one of the attending doctors tried to get us to remove the jar, since the last thing we want to do is have children associate prescription drugs with candy, but no one ever actually got around to doing it, so the candy jar remained, outlasting the doctor, who had since moved to another hospital.

On the wall behind the counter a green tinsel garland was hung in the shape of a heartbeat line. This was my original idea and contribution to the holiday decor. I was proud that it had survived four Christmases. One of the nurses was taping

Christmas cards from former patients to the wall above and below the garland.

I hummed Christmas songs as I walked around the unit. Amelia was the first to call me on it.

"You're awful jovial this morning. Emphasis on *awful*."

"What's wrong with being happy? It's a nice day."

She looked at me suspiciously. "So it seems." Her eyes narrowed. "Something's up."

"Something is definitely up." I smiled as I walked off to meet with the night shift nurse.

A new patient had come into our unit while I was off. He was a fourteen-year-old boy in the advanced stages of a neuroblastoma relapse. His name was Ryan and, other than the seriousness of his condition, all I knew about him was that he was belligerent and had bright purple hair.

The night shift nurse, Stefani, caught me up on his condition then added sarcastically, "You're going to have fun today. He keeps pulling off his pulsox."

"Pulsox" was our abbreviation for pulse oximeter, that plastic thing we clip on patients' fingers to measure oxygen saturation in their bloodstream. When it's pulled off, it sets off an alarm, which raises *our* blood pressure. "Good luck," she said with a knowing smile. It didn't take long before the alarm went off.

I walked into the room. A young man with purple hair glared angrily at me. He had dark circles under his eyes, which protruded slightly from their sockets, another gift of his condition.

"Who are you?" His voice dripped with hostility.

"I'm Richelle. But you can call me Ricki."

"Why would I do that?"

"No reason," I said. "Hey, think you could put that back on?"

"Put what on?"

He had glanced down at the pulsox, so I knew he knew what I was talking about. "The thing you just took off your finger."

"No."

"Why not?"

"It sucks."

"I know," I said. "It does suck."

He just stared at me as the alarm beeped. I walked over and turned it off, then went to the side of his bed. Even with the alarm off, the room was still noisy from the syncopated beeps from a half dozen other machines, chirping like crickets. He was just fourteen years old, with less than a 5 percent chance of living to Christmas. I couldn't blame him for being angry.

"So you dyed your hair purple," I said.

"What about it?"

"It's cool."

My response seemed to surprise him.

"What color did it used to be?"

"Red."

"So, when they colored it, did they just add blue to it, or did they just go after it with that rad purple dye? You know, just in case I decide to do it."

"It was all purple crap."

"Oh, that purple crap. Was it your idea?"

"Yeah. My mom said I could dye it if I quit calling her on her honeymoon."

"Well played," I said. "Well played. What grade are you in?"

"Ninth."

I bet your cool hair drives all the ninth-grade girls crazy. It would me."

He actually stopped frowning. "Are you Chinese or Japanese?"

"I'm half Taiwanese."

"What's Taiwanese?"

"It's Chinese."

He nodded slightly. "You're kind of hot."

I smiled. "You think so?"

He nodded again. "Do you have a boyfriend?"

"I'm kind of working on it."

"Can I have a picture with you? To show my friends."

"Are you going to post it online?"

"Yeah. Everyone will think I'm cool."

"You are cool, Ryan." I just looked at him. "You know, I'm not supposed to, but rules are made to be broken, right?"

His smile grew. "Right. Can you get close, like you were into me or something?"

"Who says I'm not?" I lifted the cell phone by his bed. "Here you go."

He unlocked his phone, then handed it back to me. "You hold it." He couldn't hold it out because of all the lines and IVs running from his arms.

I snapped several shots, then set the phone back on the stand next to his bed. "Thanks, Ryan. If it gets out there, my boyfriend will probably get jealous. You know, seeing me with a purple-haired stud like you."

He suddenly looked concerned. "He won't, like, want to beat me up, will he?"

"Nah, not a tough guy like you. So are you going to keep your hair purple or change it up from time to time?"

"I don't know. The doctor says my hair will probably start falling out."

"Well, you don't have to worry about that. You've got a great head. It's the people with ugly heads who have to cover them with hair."

"You got that right." He looked down at the pulsox lying next to him. "What does that stupid thing do anyway?"

"You mean besides suck? Well, between us, it's actually kind of cool. It emits a special ray that can pass through your skin and tissue and measure just how much oxygen is in your blood. This monitor right there then posts the numbers so we can see them. Here, watch this." I put the pulsox on my finger and the numbers on the monitor began to rise. "Pretty cool, huh?"

"Okay. I'll wear it."

I slipped the cuff back on his finger.

"You've got to keep oxygen in your blood," I said. "Otherwise, you'll turn into a zombie."

"Really?"

"No. I just made that part up. But it would be cool, wouldn't it?"

"Totally cool. When I die, I want to be a zombie. You know, the walking undead . . ."

This struck my heart. "How about you just keep living?

There's too many zombies in this world, and there's definitely not enough handsome men with purple hair to go around."

He smiled. "Okay."

"I've got to go, but I'll be back to check on you soon."

"Ricki, right?"

I smiled. "Yes. But only you can call me that. I reserve that for special people."

"Okay. You can come back whenever. Even if you just want to hang out. I'm cool with that."

"Thanks. I'd like that. Wait, you don't have a girlfriend who will beat me up, do you?"

"No."

"Okay. Then I'll be back."

I waited until I was out the door to wipe my eyes.

# CHAPTER

## *eight*

*I don't know why I must learn this lesson over and over—that*
*loneliness is more of an internal phenomenon than an external one.*
*There's nothing more lonesome than a crowd of people. After church,*
*I came home alone and self-medicated with a bowl of pralines and cream.*
*Can there really be any drug more potent than a dish of ice cream?*

*—Richelle Bach's diary*

Sunday I went to church, something I hadn't done since my father's funeral. When I was younger, this was something my father and I did together. He would always hold my hand as we walked in. Michelle never wanted to go, which meant alone time with my father. I suppose I thought going again might make me feel close to him, but seeing all the couples and families just made me feel lonely. I left before the last song ended.

I went home and sat on the couch with a bowl of pecan praline ice cream. I wondered what Justin was doing.

CHAPTER

*nine*

*I woke happy. Recklessly happy, like a cyclist speeding perilously down a steep hill. I know this thing with Justin is moving way too fast for my usually cautious self, but the thrill of the ride keeps my hand off the brake. I just hope there aren't too many rocks in the road ahead.*

*—Richelle Bach's diary*

## MONDAY, NOVEMBER 18

J ustin texted me a little after two o'clock to let me know he was back in town and looking forward to the evening. I couldn't remember the last time I had had anyone over for dinner. In spite of the fact that my diet mainly consisted of avocado toast and arugula salads, I was actually a pretty good cook, since Michelle and I had taken on the family cooking duties before we were teenagers.

As my father got sicker, I came back and cooked for him, at least until his final days when he stopped eating. I missed that time we had together. It wasn't the act of cooking—it was doing something for him. Now, by the time I got home, I was usually too tired to cook just for myself.

I decided to make a carbonara, something I used to make all the time when I was younger. I had the day off, so I went to the local Italian grocery and got cured meats and pecorino cheese; anchovies and olive oil for a Caesar salad; and a pound of spaghetti, fresh Parmesan, and pancetta for the pasta.

It was nice cooking again for someone. Aside from my father, the only other man I had ever cooked for was James, which wasn't exactly rewarding, since he was an incredibly picky eater and would point out the deficits in my cooking. Once I made a meal that he took one look at, then suggested we go out for dinner. I don't know why I put up with that. I guess it was the pleaser in me. I wondered if Justin was like that. He was a rocket scientist, so I assumed he had to be precise, which is usually just another word for picky. Still, no one shows that side of themselves on a first date, at least, not if they're hoping for a second one. I found myself thinking about the kiss and how beautiful it felt. I hoped there would be more tonight.

Justin arrived at my house a couple minutes before seven. I didn't hear him knock the first time since I was in the bathroom blow-drying my hair. A few minutes later I saw his text come over my phone.

**JUSTIN**

Anybody home?

"Sorry about that," I said, opening the door. "I was still getting ready."

He was holding a bottle of wine in one hand and a bouquet of flowers in the other.

"No worries," he said. "Anticipation has always been the better part of pleasure." He handed me the bouquet. It was made up of white roses with blue delphinium and Peruvian lilies. *White* roses. I had never really liked red roses. I thought they were clichéd. Of course, it had been so long since anyone had given me anything growing—other than a virus—that I wouldn't have objected to poison ivy and thistle.

"How did you know that I liked white roses?"

"Red just felt unoriginal," he said.

"I know, right?"

He held up the bottle of wine. "I also brought matching wine. It's a pinot grigio. Hopefully it will go with dinner. Whatever you're making, it smells exquisite."

*Exquisite.* I smiled at the word. "Thank you. It's Italian again. I'll chill this and put these in water. You can have a seat in the living room. There's some antipasto on the table."

"Thank you."

I put the wine in the fridge and the flowers in a crystal vase, then put the vase on the kitchen table. Justin was sitting on the couch. He had balanced a cracker with cheese and a slice of salami.

"I love your home," he said.

"It was my father's. He left it to me when he passed." I stopped myself from explaining. "You can tell it's older. Post–World War Two. People don't build homes this small anymore."

"They're too busy building monuments to themselves."

My father had once said that. "You're probably right. I hope you're hungry."

"Famished. All I've had today are the peanuts and Biscoff cookies on the plane."

"Eating healthy, I see. Come on in."

He followed me into the small dining room. I had brought out my father's lace tablecloth, fancy china and silverware, something I hadn't done in years. In the center of the table I had put two candlesticks in a crystal candelabra. We sat down across from each other.

"Would you like some wine?" Justin asked.

"Yes, I put it in the fridge. I'll get it."

Justin stood. "I'll get it." He got up and walked into the kitchen.

"Oh, you'll need the corkscrew. It's in the drawer . . ." He walked out with the bottle in one hand and the corkscrew in the other. "You found it."

"It wasn't hard." He opened the bottle and poured my glass, then his. "How long have you lived in this house?"

"Forever," I said. "Almost forever. Up until graduate school. It's a little strange coming back to the house I was raised in. There's still a lot of my father here."

"Is that good or bad?"

"Both. It's good that it reminds me of him. Bad that it reminds me that he isn't here."

Justin nodded knowingly. "It's a cruel blessing to have had someone in your life to miss so badly." The moment fell into silence. Justin said, "Why do you think your father never remarried?"

"I asked him that once. He said, 'Because I already have two precious ladies in my life.' " I sighed. "Ironically, a few months before he died, he asked me why I wasn't married. I said, 'Because I already have the best man in my life.' He said, 'Only for a little while longer, sweetheart.' " I took a sip of wine. "He taught me the meaning of love."

What I said seemed to affect him. He asked softly, "And what is the meaning of love?"

"To love someone is to desire their happiness," I said.

Again there was silence. Then he said, "We should toast to that." He raised his glass. "To love. And to your father, who understood it."

I lifted my glass as well. "To Dad."

We clinked our glasses, then drank.

"Thank you." I gathered myself, then said, "Well, let's eat. Let me dish this up for you." I stood up and filled his plate with pasta. He waited until I sat back down then swirled some noodles around his fork and took a bite. I could tell from his expression that he liked it.

"Exquisite," he said again.

"You're overselling it."

"I don't think so. Do you cook often?"

"I used to, but now that it's just me, I hardly ever do. It seems like every time I start planning dinner, I think, 'Why bother?' and make myself some toast."

He laughed. "I get it. I've taken to eating toaster strudels, ramen, and street tacos."

"I love street tacos," I said. "During the summer there's this guy with a taco cart on the corner of Fifty-Fourth and State.

The PICU staff takes turns making runs there. Of course, in Utah, the taco carts all disappear in the winter."

"Didn't have that problem in California," Justin said. "I'm not sure about adjusting to the cold here."

"The snow is pretty, but the cold and ice can take some getting used to. You have to have the right blood for it."

"You mean antifreeze?"

"Something like that."

"Do you ski?"

"I used to. My dad would take us girls every weekend. Michelle was really good. She was fearless. She liked to ski the black diamonds. Then she started snowboarding. I never switched over. Then I moved to Texas . . ."

"Not a lot of skiing in Texas."

"No. Then after I came back, I just never got back into it."

"So what do you do for fun?"

I honestly couldn't come up with anything. "It seems like work is the only thing I really do these days."

His brow furrowed. "Why is that?"

I shook my head. "I don't know. My supervisor brought me in to ask me that. She's afraid I'm going to burn out."

"Do you go out much with friends?"

"Not really. All my friends are either out of state or work at the hospital with me. Sometimes we'll go out to dinner after work, but usually we're all just tired and can't wait to get home."

"What about your friends in your writers group?"

"Outside of our meetings, I never see any of them." I looked at him dully. "I know, I sound pathetic. How about you?"

"Almost the same. My close friends all live out of state."

"Do you still connect with any of them?"

"My best friend is still my brother," he said. "But there's a group from high school I still keep in touch with. We go up to Alaska once a year to go salmon and halibut fishing. It's amazing, because I don't see these guys all year, then it's like we just take up where we left off."

"Do you have friends from work?"

"I don't know if I'd call them friends. I liked my colleagues. We'd occasionally get a drink after work, like after we'd finished a big project or to celebrate something, but other than that we never really hung out. The thing is, it's different when you're married. Once you have someone to go home to, it changes things."

"I discovered that from the other side," I said. "After my friends got married, they stopped calling. So, now that you're single again, what now?"

"I'm just trying to figure it all out. Do I turn the page or start a new book?"

"Nice writer's metaphor," I said.

We ate for a few more minutes, and then Justin said, "Tell me about your opal necklace."

I touched it. "It's a black opal. My father gave it to me for my high school graduation. He gave one to both my sister and me."

"Black opals are valuable."

"Very," I said. "I had it appraised a couple years ago for my insurance company. It was worth almost fifteen thousand dollars."

"May I see it?"

"Sure." I unclasped the necklace from my neck and held it out to him by its chain. He took it from me, carefully analyzing the stone. "It's beautiful. The fire is green and blue." After a moment he handed it back. "I love opals."

I clasped the necklace back around my neck. "My father said he got them for my sister and me because they looked identical, but each had its own unique fire. Like us."

"Your father had a poetic spirit."

"Very much so. He saw the connection between things. He always wanted to be a writer. He had the same name as a famous writer."

"Richard Bach," he said. *"Jonathan Livingston Seagull."*

I nodded. People, at least older people, asked me all the time if he was the writer. They always seemed disappointed when I told them he wasn't.

"He even wrote a screenplay once, but he never did anything with it. Wasted dreams, I suppose."

"I don't think there's such a thing," Justin said. "Dreams have value in themselves." He looked at me softly. "Tell me about your dreams."

No one had ever asked me that before. Not even James. I had to think about it. "I dream of being a successful author."

"That's a good dream. Anything else?"

"Anything else." I sighed. "I used to have dreams by the boatload. One by one they all just slipped away. Life has a way of stealing our dreams."

He frowned. "Tell me about your stolen dreams."

"My biggest dreams were actually the simplest ones. I wanted someone to live my life with. I wanted children. I wanted to grow old with someone." I wondered if that would scare him. "That probably sounds boring to you."

"No, that sounds meaningful. What happened to that dream?"

"I don't know." I breathed out slowly. "Too much pain followed it."

He suddenly looked contemplative. "Even if we get our dream, it doesn't mean it will last. I learned that the hard way." He sighed lightly. "The price of love is the risk of losing it."

I frowned. "Is it worth the risk?"

"I've thought a lot about that. I still think the greatest hurt isn't to lose love, it's the regret of never having it. To have never felt love, that would be true tragedy."

For the first time in a long time I felt like I was talking with someone who understood me. I wanted to open up more to him. "You asked why my sister and I stopped talking."

"We don't have to talk about that right now."

"I want to. I think you'll understand."

He sat back in his chair. "All right."

"So, after high school, I worked a little, then started college. My sister, Michelle, asked our father for her inheritance so she could run off to Europe with some guy she barely knew."

"That sounds a little like your book," he said.

"It's *a lot* like my book," I said. "My father gave up almost half of his retirement money. I resented Michelle for that. My father didn't even want her to go, but he believed in letting us make our own choices. Even bad ones."

"What happened?"

"No surprise, the guy was a train wreck. He took all her

money and left her penniless in Warsaw, of all places. She had to call my father for money to come home.

"But instead of coming home, she landed in Milan, where she got a job with a high-fashion clothing designer. I have no idea how she got the job, but I wasn't completely surprised. Michelle could talk her way into almost anything."

"She definitely looked the part of a fashion model," Justin said.

"How do you know what she looked—" I stopped myself. "Thank you."

He smiled.

". . . Like I said, she could talk her way into things. And out of them. The last week of our senior year of high school, Michelle came to me crying. She said she couldn't pass her math class without doing well on her final, and there was no way she was going to pass it. She said that if she didn't pass her math class, she wouldn't graduate.

"I offered to tutor her, but she just said, 'You think I'm going to learn an entire year of math in one night? I'm not you.' I asked her what she wanted me to do. She said, 'I want you to take my final for me. No one will know. This would be so easy for you.' She was right on both counts. None of our teachers could tell us apart, and Michelle was only taking basic algebra, while I was getting As in advanced calculus. She just kept saying, 'You're just so much smarter than me.' I told her that cheating would be wrong. She said, 'And not helping your sister is *right*?'

"She knew exactly where to hit me, since I always felt protective of her. I said, 'You know, I could be expelled for helping you.'

"She said, 'It's the last week of school; they're not going to expel anyone. Especially you. No one would even believe you would do it. But just to be safe, we'll wear the same outfit that day. That way they can never prove it.'

"I had to admit it was a pretty good plan," I said. "Then she delivered the coup de grâce: 'We have the same DNA; that means we're the same person. You're really just doing it for yourself.' "

"That's a clever argument," Justin said. "What did you do?"

"I did what I always did when Michelle wanted something. I caved. Taking the test was kind of a bizarre experience. I had to chew gum the whole time, since that's what Michelle did. The test was easy. I had to intentionally answer some of the questions wrong so it wouldn't look too obvious. You have no idea how hard that was for me. I could have completed it in ten minutes, but that would have looked suspicious, so I just sat there. I was the last one to turn in my test.

"After class her teacher collared me. At first I was panicked. I was sure he'd figured out that I wasn't really Michelle. But he hadn't. Instead, he wanted to give me a lecture. He told me that if I'd just applied myself more, I could have done well in his class. Then he asked me why I wasn't more like my sister."

"What did you say to that?"

"I said, 'Because I'm not my sister.' "

Justin looked amused. "In a way, you told him the truth, and he never realized it. Did anyone else suspect you weren't Michelle?"

"I think some of her friends knew I wasn't her, but no one said anything. She got an A minus on the test—at least, *I* got an A minus—and that's how my sister graduated from high school."

"Was she grateful?"

"She thanked me, but I think part of her resented me for it." I sighed. ". . . So back to Europe. Michelle was still in Italy when I started nursing school in Texas. That's where I met James. He was getting his MBA. He was kind of a big deal. He was the president of the MBA student association and was being scouted by some pretty major investment firms.

"I was sure he was the one. You know, he checked off all the boxes on my list. He was smart, handsome, ambitious, he came from a good family. Six months later we were engaged. I felt lucky. My dreams were rolling out just the way I'd imagined them. I remember fantasizing about what our children would look like.

"The winter I finished school, I told my father that James and I would be coming home for Christmas. My father was ecstatic. Then he told me that he had more good news. Michelle would be there too. Even though we texted a lot, I hadn't seen her for more than four years. I was really excited to see her.

"James and I arrived in Salt Lake the middle of December. Dad and Michelle picked us up at the airport. You should have seen James's face when he saw her. Just imagine seeing an exact replica of someone you knew. I had warned him it might be a little weird, but until you actually see someone's *double*, you're not really prepared for it."

"I can imagine," Justin said. "So how did things go? Being with your sister again."

"Wonderfully, at first. The next week was perfect. We all stayed together here, in the house. My father loved Christmas. So, of course, he had the home all decorated. Except he saved the tree for us to decorate together. The four of us just spent our time together, talking, eating, laughing, telling jokes. It was perfect.

"The stories Michelle told about her life would be unbelievable for anyone else, but not her. I mean, the Italian men chasing her, wardrobe malfunctions at Milan Fashion Week. She had changed from the lost little girl who had run off into a confident, powerful woman. She had come into her own. She seemed happy, for once.

"Outside of a few tattoos she'd added, we were still identical. We laughed the same, talked the same, had the same mannerisms. I think I'd forgotten how alike we were. Twice James mistook Michelle for me, once coming up behind her and kissing her on the neck."

Justin's eyebrows rose. "You're sure that was an accident?"

I shrugged. "He said it was. I don't know why I believed him. The thing was, I felt close to my sister again. I remember thinking that it was one of the best weeks of my life."

I exhaled slowly. "All that changed in an instant. One evening my father took me downtown to see the Christmas lights. He wanted to take all of us, but Michelle had a migraine, and then James said he was tired and suggested that it might be nice if my father and I just took the night for ourselves. Honestly, I thought that was a good idea too.

"We had a beautiful time. We had dinner at one of my father's favorite old restaurants. We walked around Temple

Square, bought saltwater taffy, then went to a little coffee shop and got hot cocoa. It was just like when I was a child. I realized how much I had missed him. We talked about deep things, like we always did. He asked me candid questions about James, like, was I certain that he was the one. What a question, right? I told him I had never been so certain about anything in my life.

"When we got home, my father went to bed. I went to check on Michelle to see how she was feeling, but she wasn't in her room. Then I went down to my room. I found her in bed with James."

Justin just frowned. "I'm sorry."

"I honestly can't tell you how long it took for me to put together what I was seeing. It's amazing how the brain works in moments of crisis."

"Like a car accident," Justin said.

"Just like a car accident. Except worse. Time froze. At first I told myself, James must think it's me. It was stupid, but the ego does what it has to to protect itself. But from the look in his eyes, it was obvious he knew better.

"When I finally let it sink in, I went crazy. I started screaming. I kicked James out of the house. After he was gone, I just looked at Michelle. She was sobbing. All I could say was, 'Why?' She wouldn't look at me." I stopped, overcome with emotion. "She packed up her things and left. The last thing I said to her was, 'I never want to see you again.' " I breathed out heavily. "I guess you should be careful what you wish for.

"That was the last time I saw her. She didn't even say goodbye to Dad. I had to tell him what had happened."

"How did he take it?"

"Not well. He wept. I think for both of us."

Justin just slowly shook his head. "I'm sorry," he said again.

"For the longest time, I just couldn't make sense of it. Why would James cheat on me? I mean, sometimes it's obvious, right? Man falls for someone younger or hotter, but we were completely identical, so it couldn't have been the looks.

"The truth is, it shouldn't have been so hard to figure out; I just didn't want to see the truth. He didn't want boring, predictable me. He wanted someone exciting like Michelle."

". . . Or maybe he was just a creep," Justin said.

I didn't know what to say to that. Finally I said, "It took me a while to realize that Michelle's betrayal was worse than James's. For most of our lives we'd been inseparable. Even when she was in Europe we texted almost every day." I took another breath. "Two weeks later I found out that James and Michelle had shacked up together in California. It didn't last long. When it came to men, Michelle was catch-and-release. She said she'd never marry, and she never did. After James was gone, she went through a slew of other boy toys. At least, that's what I saw online."

Justin's brow furrowed. "You followed her on social media?"

"Just for a few months or so. And not every day, just in my weaker moments. At least until I realized I was only hurting myself and let her go.

"I almost called her when my father died. *Almost*. What a word. I should have called her." I shook my head. "She didn't even come to the funeral. Part of me was glad. I didn't want to see her, and I still hadn't forgiven her for what she'd done to me or my father." My eyes moistened. "He was so good to her. He was always so good to her." I covered my eyes with my hand. Justin put his arms around me. When I finally looked back up I could see that his eyes were moist as well. Still he said nothing.

"I'm sorry. I just vomited all that up."

"It's all right." There was a long pause, then he said, "The deathbed promise you mentioned. Was that to your father?"

I slowly nodded. "I suppose there were two of them. A couple of months before he died, I asked him what he wanted for Christmas. He said not to worry because he probably wouldn't be around for Christmas. I hated hearing that. Then he said, 'I want something from you.' I asked him what. He got emotional, something he rarely did. He said, 'Losing your mother really did a number on my heart. It made me too afraid to try again. Promise me that you won't be a coward like me and give up on love. Promise me that.' "

"The reason he didn't remarry was because your mother broke his heart?"

I slowly nodded. "I don't know how I missed that."

"What was the second promise?"

"It was less than a week before he died. I was caring for him at home. He had a really high fever and I'd been patting his forehead with a wet cloth. Suddenly he opened his eyes and just looked at me. Then he said, 'It's been long enough, Ricki. You need to forgive your sister.' Then he closed his eyes again. It's one of the last coherent things he said."

I slowly shook my head. "I promised him I would. But I never did. And now it's too late."

We both were quiet again, then Justin said, "You've been through too much. Would it be okay if I just held you?"

"I'd like that."

He took my hand and led me to the sofa. He walked over and closed the front window curtains, then came back and sat down next to me. "Come here," he said.

I lay my head on his shoulder, and he put his arms around me. "Everything will be okay," he whispered. He kissed the top of my head, then leaned back and wrapped both arms around me as I sank into him. I had never told anyone so much about my betrayal. I should have felt raw and vulnerable. I suppose I did, but more than that I felt safe. It was a peculiar emotional balancing act. I fell asleep listening to his heartbeat.

It was dark when I woke; the room's only light was the illumination from the stove's light in the kitchen. Justin's fingers were gently kneading my hair. I looked up at him. There was nothing I could have said that would have added anything. He looked down at me with soft, haunting eyes, the same way he had looked at me in the parking lot the first time we kissed. We kissed again.

# CHAPTER

*ten*

*Today Justin and I dressed the house for the holidays.*
*What a sweet combination—a new friend and old traditions.*
*It's like drinking a fresh cup of coffee from*
*a favorite old cup.*
*—Richelle Bach's diary*

J ustin left my house sometime after one. As late as it was, I couldn't sleep. I just lay there thinking about him, the depth of the things we'd talked about, the depth of his kisses. I could still smell his cologne on me. It was a deep musky scent, masculine. That's what I finally fell asleep to. I woke the next morning to a text message.

**JUSTIN**

What are we doing today?

A smile crossed my lips. I texted back.

Come over for coffee.

He texted me a thumbs-up emoji. Not a minute later my doorbell rang. I got out of bed, still in my pink leopard-print pajamas, and looked out the peephole. It was Justin.

"You texted me from my driveway?" I asked, opening the door.

"I just happened to be in the neighborhood . . ." He looked me up and down. "Nice pajamas."

I grabbed his arm, grinning. "Come in, it's cold."

"Is it ever warm here?"

"Sometimes." I shut the door behind him. "What did you do, sleep in your car?"

"No. Or you would have found me frozen to death. I actually went home." He looked down at himself. "See, not the same clothes."

"And I'm wearing my pajamas. Sit down, I'll put some clothes on."

"Where's this coffee you lured me here with?"

"Sorry, I didn't have time to make it on the way to answer the doorbell. It usually takes more than ten seconds."

"I'll make it. Where do you keep your coffee?"

"It's in the cupboard left of the oven."

"I'm on it."

I went into my bedroom and changed into some jeans and a sweater. I put on a little mascara and lipstick. When I came back out Justin was sitting at the table with two coffee cups.

"How do you like your coffee?"

"With milk," I said.

"I'll get it." He got a milk carton from the fridge, poured a little into my cup, and then handed the cup to me.

"Thank you," I said.

He sat down across from me. "You're welcome."

"And thank you for last night. It was healing to finally share that with someone."

"Thank you for trusting me." He took a drink of his coffee. "That was a little intense. Maybe we should have a lighter day today."

"What do you have in mind?"

"Well, you said you loved Christmas, but I don't see any evidence."

"I've been busy."

"No shame," he said. "I just think we should bring Christmas back to this house."

"I like that idea."

"Good. We'll start with the tree. I passed a tree lot on the way here."

"I'll get my coat."

━━━━━━

The Christmas tree lot Justin had referred to had sprung up the first day of November in the corner of the parking lot of the Albertsons grocery store where I shopped.

After a lecture from the tree lot guy on the merits of the different kinds of trees, we settled on a cone-shaped blue spruce that was a foot taller than me. We tied it to the top of my car with twine, then drove it home.

I set up our old metal tree stand, then we carried the tree inside. We went downstairs to the furnace room and carried up three dusty plastic bins filled with my father's Christmas decorations.

"These are cool," Justin said, lifting one of the vintage ornaments from its wrapping. "Are they antiques?"

"Some of them are. My father would buy us a new ornament every year. Usually from a different country."

We carefully unwrapped all the ornaments, then laid them out on the carpet around the tree. Foraging through the boxes of decorations I found a small plastic Santa Claus face with a red felt hat and cotton-ball beard. It was attached to a toothpick. I held it up for Justin to see.

"Michelle and I used to take turns hiding this in the tree. We'd time each other, then add up how long it took to find it. I was really good at hiding things, so I always won. Michelle would get so mad. Once she was so angry she threw a bauble at the wall and shattered it."

"Did she get punished?"

"No. It was her ornament, so that was sort of a punishment in itself."

"So where do we begin decorating?"

"There's a process to this," I said. "My father always did things by the book."

"I haven't read that book," Justin said. "So, you'll have to tell me what to do."

"First, we hang the lights."

"That makes sense, since it's not easy putting the lights up over the ornaments. And the odds of breaking them are much higher."

"Spoken like a rocket scientist," I said. "And, the light cord gives us something extra to hang the ornaments from. But before we string up the lights, we must—"

"Light a candle."

I looked at him. "Light a candle?"

"I'm just guessing," he said.

I smiled. "It's something much more practical. I'm a little surprised a rocket scientist missed it. We need to check the lights to make sure they work."

"I was just about to suggest that."

"I'm sure you were."

"Seriously, I was." He took one end of the strand and plugged it into the socket next to the tree. They lit up. "They work."

"That's all you got, rocket scientist? They work?"

"All systems go," he said.

"Much better. On to phase two, wrapping the lights." I helped him drape the lights around the tree. As we finished I said, "Wait, we're missing something." I walked into my father's room, went to the closet, and brought back a box of albums. I lifted one of the albums out of the box. "We decorated to this every year."

"An album? You still have a record player?"

"Technically it's an RCA Hi-Fi console. Dad loved tech, except when it came to music. He was a vinyl purist." I walked over to the cabinet, carefully removed the album from its sleeve, and set it over the spindle. Then I turned on the carousel and set the needle down. It crackled briefly, and then music filled the room.

Justin stopped what he was doing and looked at me. "Wait,

I know this." A few more bars played. "This is the music from the Charlie Brown Christmas show."

I tapped my nose, then pointed at him like we were playing charades. "Vince Guaraldi. *A Charlie Brown Christmas*. The ultimate in Christmas iconography."

"How could you not be happy listening to this?"

"You can't, right? It's like ear candy." I walked back over to the tree.

"Now the ornaments?" Justin asked.

"There's an order to that too."

"Of course there is," he said.

"At least the first two. The first is this one." I took out an ornament that was still in the bin and unwrapped it. It was a cross made of two rough nails with a red ribbon for hanging. Printed on the ribbon were the words *John 3:16* and *Luke 2:10–11*.

I recited the verses. "John 3:16: 'For God so loved the world that He gave His only begotten Son, that whosoever believes in Him should not perish but have everlasting life.' Luke 2:10–11: 'Do not be afraid, for behold, I bring you good tidings of great joy which will be to all people. For there is born to you this day in the city of David a Savior, who is Christ the Lord.' "

I looked at him. "My father said this ornament was so we wouldn't forget the reason we were celebrating Christmas. It was always the first ornament we put up and the last we'd take down."

"I'm gathering that your father was big on gestures. Like your necklaces."

"He was very big on gestures," I said. "Kind of a modern-day Cyrano de Bergerac." I looked back over at the bin. "All right, we've still got work to do. The second ornament is this one." I lifted a red gift box from the bin and pried off its lid. Inside was a bird's nest.

"When Michelle and I were five, my dad let us pick out the tree. When we got it home, we discovered that there was a bird's nest in it.

"My father told us it was a cardinal's nest. He said the cardinal is a symbol of hope, so it would be wrong to take hope from our tree, so we left it there. After Christmas, my father put it in this box, and we've put it back up every year since." I smiled at the memory. "Michelle and I secretly believed that if we wished hard enough, someday the bird would come back to it. Sometimes we would sit on the couch and wait for it. I don't know how we thought it would come into the house. We left the door open once, but my dad got mad that we'd let all the cold in. Michelle said that if Santa could get in, the bird could too."

"Smart girl," Justin said.

"I have such fond memories of Christmas. My father believed that tradition was important. He said it was the foundation of home and culture."

"I think he's right," Justin said. "It's how a culture is developed. In families as well as in the world."

"What were your family's traditions?"

"My parents both have Swedish ancestry, so we pretty much followed all the Swedish customs, with a few American adaptations. We'd start our celebration by lighting a candle on Advent Sunday, then an additional candle every Sunday until Christmas. My mother would make pepparkakor gingerbread cookies. Pepparkakor cookies are heart-shaped, and my mother taught us to hold the cookie in the palm of our hand and then break it with the knuckle of our other hand. If it broke into three pieces, you would give the largest piece to the person you loved.

"I'd go through a dozen cookies to get one to break in three. Not that it was a problem, since I got to eat all the cookies I broke."

"If it broke in three, who would you give the largest piece to?" I asked.

"Myself, of course," he said, smiling. "I was a kid.

"The most non-American part of our tradition was not waking up to Santa. We'd open our presents on Christmas Eve. Then there was always a large meal. My parents called it a *julbord*, which means Christmas table. Americans think of it as the Swedish smorgasbord. We'd have smoked salmon, pickled herring and lye fish, ham, sausages, ribs, cabbage, potatoes, and—my personal favorite—Swedish meatballs.

"As a finale, my mother would bring out a rice pudding, the *risgrynsgröt*. She'd put one almond in the dish. Whoever found the almond in their bowl would have good luck throughout the year."

"All this talk of food reminds me, we're forgetting the hot cocoa. My dad was big on that. I'll make the cocoa; you can start hanging the rest of the ornaments."

"Do they go on in any particular order?"

"No. Once we got the first two on, Michelle and I would see who could put the most on fastest."

"Was everything a competition between you two?"

"Almost," I said.

I went into the kitchen and put some water on to boil. Fortunately, there was still cocoa left in the tin near the back of the cupboard. There was also an older package of marshmallows. They were hard but not stale.

"Marshmallows?" I asked.

"Yes, please."

I stirred the marshmallows into the cocoa until they dissolved, then brought our mugs out to the coffee table.

I helped Justin finish putting up the rest of the ornaments. Then we draped the tree with tinsel and sat back on the couch and sipped cocoa as we looked at what we'd created. By then the music had stopped playing.

"We need another record," I said.

"What else do you have?"

"The greats. Bing Crosby. Gene Autry. Mitch Miller. Burl Ives."

"The way Christmas music should be. Let's do Bing."

I put the record on, and the deep, mellow baritone of Bing Crosby's "White Christmas" filled the room. I came back to the couch and lay my head against Justin's shoulder. "Why does everything feel so right with you? You just feel comfortable. Like an old shoe."

"You're comparing me to an old shoe?"

"A comfortable one."

He looked at me with a crooked smile. "An old shoe."

"You know how when you get a new pair of shoes they're uncomfortable and stiff at first. You don't feel like that. You feel . . . comfortable."

"If that's the best you got, I'll take it."

"Good. It's a compliment." I took another sip of cocoa.

"What else did you do to celebrate Christmas?" he asked.

"After we decorated, my father would take us to the store to pick out a toy for a needy child. He always said, 'Christmas is about giving. And you should always give before you receive.'"

"I'm starting to think your father was a saint."

"I wondered too, and then he would hammer his thumb." I smiled sadly. "I wish you had met him."

Justin just nodded.

After we finished our drinks, we wrapped a bright red flannel skirt around the tree, then put up a wooden crèche that my father had brought back from Taiwan. There were Chinese characters engraved on the bottom of each of the figurines. I had no idea what they said, but I always thought that was cool.

"My father said, 'When people see the MADE IN TAIWAN tag on things, they wrongly think that there's some big factory pumping things out. But usually, it's just a neighborhood and a bunch of old ladies working in their homes piecing together parts. When they've filled a box they take it to their neighbor next door to complete the next part.'

"He said he once came across a small country town that exclusively made Christmas decorations. All year long it was filled with Christmas. That's where he bought this crèche."

"Did you have a Chinese name?"

I nodded. "Chen Mei Hwa. Chen was my mother's surname. Mei Hwa means beautiful flower."

"Fitting," he said. "Did you ever learn to speak Chinese?"

"Not much. My mom left when I was three. My father could speak and read enough to get by. For a while he thought it might be a good idea to have us take Chinese lessons, but it didn't take. Michelle and I were struggling enough with our identity as Asian Americans. When you're young you don't want to be different, so we sort of rebelled. All I remember is *ni hau ma*, how are you, and *wo ai ni*. It means—"

"I love you," he said.

"You knew that?"

"It's about the extent of my Chinese."

"I only remember that because my father said it to us every night when he put us to bed."

It was past noon when we finished decorating. Justin asked, "Are we going to the writers group tonight?"

I liked that he'd said "we." Frankly, I was surprised that he even remembered. "Do you want to go?"

"Only if you do."

"It's kind of my thing."

"Then we'll go. I should probably get a few things done beforehand. How about I pick you up at five thirty, we'll get some dinner, and then hit the group?"

"Sounds perfect." I walked him to the door. "Thank you again for today."

He leaned forward and kissed me. "My pleasure. And Merry Christmas."

It looked like it would be.

CHAPTER

*eleven*

*Justin and I went to the writers group tonight. Marjorie was obviously not happy to find that Justin and I are still together. I'm sure she can't imagine why he would pick me over her. I suppose it's a glimpse into my own insecurity that I've wondered the same.*

　　　　　　　　　　　　—Richelle Bach's diary

On the way to the writers group Justin asked, "Do you know what the topic of discussion is tonight?"

"No. It's always a surprise. We just know whose turn it is to lead. Tonight it's Marjorie."

"Which one is she?"

"She's the hot little blonde who has a thing for you."

He smiled. "You sound jealous."

"I'm not answering that. But I'm guessing her topic will have something to do with finding the perfect male protagonist."

The group was smaller than the week before. The regulars were there, except for Becky, whom I figured had been offended again. I wondered how long her hiatus would be this time. To my relief, Marjorie's chosen topic was how to research your writing. She basically spent the session asking everyone to share their thoughts on research (yes, it's important) and how they did it (Google).

Marjorie never once looked at me, making it clear that she was still upset that I was with Justin.

Frankly, it was one of those discussions that made me question if our group had run the extent of its purposefulness, which then made me question what its purposefulness even was.

I realized that my joining the writers group had less to do with the art of writing than it had with being alone. Calliope was the only nonwork gathering I had in my life—the only people I talked to who weren't wearing scrubs or hospital gowns. Now that I was with Justin, the whole thing seemed superfluous. I just wanted to be with him, and now I found myself wishing that we had just stayed back at my place.

Our meeting ended early, as Fred was the only one with something he wanted to share from his book, which involved the bad guys blowing up the White House while his protagonist saved the bombshell press secretary.

As we drove home Justin said, "I don't think Marjorie's very happy we're together."

"What was your first clue?" I asked sardonically.

"When she looked directly at me and said that men should do more research when creating a female lead."

"Yeah, that was a little weird."

Justin turned to me. "Would you like to do something tomorrow?"

"Of course. What do you have in mind?" Suddenly I remembered that I had committed to work for someone. I groaned. "I forgot, I have to work tomorrow."

I could see the disappointment on his face. "I thought you said you were off."

"I did. I forgot that a couple of weeks ago I told one of the nurses that I'd work for her. Her brother's getting married. That was before . . ." I breathed out heavily. "I could try to back out."

"If it's her brother's wedding, she'd never forgive you. I'll come over when you're done. We can go get some dinner. Or whatever."

"Maybe dinner *and* whatever," I said as we pulled into my driveway. "I don't work Thursday. If you want to spend it with me."

"Of course I do. We'll spend the whole day together."

"Do you have to leave Friday afternoon?"

"I'm flying out in the morning," he said. "With Thanksgiving coming up, I need to get back a little earlier this weekend."

He walked me to my front door. I unlocked it, then asked, "Do you want to come in?"

He hesitated a moment, then said, "No. You have an early day tomorrow, and I don't want you falling asleep on me tomorrow night."

"I love falling asleep on you."

He smiled. "You know what I mean."

I leaned into him and we kissed. When I finally stopped kissing him, I said, "Are you sure?"

"You better get your sleep," he said.

"All right." We kissed once more, then I went into the house. "Good night."

"Night." I watched as he walked to his car.

As he drove away, I realized that I didn't feel lonely anymore. And I didn't feel so cold.

# CHAPTER

*twelve*

*There's still more snow. It feels like the universe's commentary on my emotional state. I had a very uncomfortable lunch at the cafeteria with Amelia and Camille. I don't know if the problem was that they asked too many hard questions or that I didn't. There's so much I don't know about Justin. I guess when something looks delicious, we're less inclined to check the ingredients.*

*—Richelle Bach's Diary*

## WEDNESDAY, NOVEMBER 20

The snow the next morning was relentless, paving the streets in solid white sheets. I wondered if I'd even be able to get my car out of the garage. It was the first time in a long time that I didn't want to go to work. On the drive in I decided that the first thing I was going to do was ask for Thanksgiving off.

"Man, that's a beastly snow," Amelia said as I walked into

the unit. "We passed like six cars off the road on the way here."

"We?"

"Yeah, I've been carpooling with Guy."

I was surprised that she was still with him. Maybe she really did like him but didn't want to admit it. "Really? How's that going?"

"It's going. I just wish they'd build a covered parking lot for employees. I feel like I need a dog sled just to get from my car to the hospital."

"You could have had Guy drop you off at the curb."

"Yeah, I thought of that. But he pouts if I don't hold his hand."

"Good luck with that," I said. "It's too bad the hospital isn't like school, so they could cancel it when there's too much snow."

"Maybe people should just stop getting sick."

"If only," I said. "Did you see if Terri was in her office?"

"When is she not?"

"Thanks."

I went to Terri's office and knocked on the door.

"Come in."

Terri looked up at me from her computer. "Hi, Richelle. What's up?"

"I've been thinking about what you said, and I think I'd like to have Thanksgiving off."

"I'm glad you told me that today, because I was just about to send out the schedule, and I hate hearing people whine about working holidays."

"They'll still whine," I said.

"Yes, but it's easier to not give a dog a bone than it is to take it away from her."

"Thanks, Terri," I said.

"You're welcome. I'm glad you came to your senses."

———

A little after noon I went down to the cafeteria for lunch with Amelia and a new nurse named Camille, who had joined the PICU just three months earlier. We all got salads, then sat down near one of the windows. We were lucky to get a table since the place was slammed. With the storm like it was, no one was leaving the hospital to eat.

"Look at that snow keep coming," Amelia said. "By the time we get off, we're going to need ice picks to unbury our cars."

"I thought the world was supposed to be warming," Camille said. "It's like we're entering a new ice age. I hate driving in this."

"At least Amelia doesn't have to anymore," I said.

"Why is that?"

"She's got a new boyfriend-chauffeur."

"He's not a boyfriend," Amelia said. "He's a ride."

She turned to me. "Speaking of men, tell us about the new man in your life." A few days earlier I had told Amelia that I'd spent the day with Justin.

"What do you want to know?" I asked.

"Is he from Salt Lake?" Camille asked.

"He's from California. He just moved here."

"Where did you meet?"

"At my writers group."

"So he's an author too."

"Sort of. He hasn't written anything yet."

"He's an author without a book," said Camille. "Like a fish without a bicycle."

"That doesn't make sense," I said. "Besides, I'm an author without a book."

"Do you have a picture of him?" Amelia asked.

"Yes." I took out my phone and showed them the picture that we'd taken inside the Tuscany restaurant.

"He's a hottie," Camille said.

I smiled. "I know."

"What does he do for work?" Camille asked.

"He's a rocket scientist."

"He's gorgeous *and* he's a rocket scientist," Camille said incredulously. "He sounds like a character from one of my romance novels."

"That does seem a little suspect," Amelia said. "Is that what he said?"

"What he said is, he's an aerospace engineer."

Amelia looked skeptical. "And you believe him?"

My eyes darted back and forth between them. "Why wouldn't I?"

"Does Utah even have rockets?" Camille asked.

"He's not here for work," I said.

"Why is he here?" Amelia asked.

To my surprise I couldn't answer her. "I feel like I'm being interrogated."

"You're not being interrogated, we're just watching out for you," Amelia said. "There are a lot of weirdos out there."

"He's not a weirdo."

"No one thinks they're with a weirdo," Camille said, "or they wouldn't be with them."

"Good point," Amelia said. "Where does he live?"

"I don't know. I've never been to his place."

Camille frowned. "What does he drive?"

"What does that matter?"

"What a person drives says a lot about them."

Now I really didn't want to tell them.

"What is it, a beater?"

"It changes every time. He drives a rental car."

"A rental car," Camille repeated.

"Has he ever been married?" Amelia asked.

"Now you *are* interrogating me. He just got divorced, all right? That's why he's taking a sabbatical right now."

Amelia's brow fell. "I'm sorry, but doesn't it seem . . . *sketchy?*"

"What seems sketchy?"

"I'm just seeing a whole field of red flags here. He's an author but doesn't have a book, he's a rocket scientist but he's unemployed and living someplace without rockets. He drives a rental car and has never invited you to his house. That doesn't seem sketchy?"

"You're making him sound like a serial killer. What do you think he's doing?"

"I have no idea. It just seems . . ."

"Sketchy," I said. "I know, you've said it."

"We're just watching out for you," Camille said. "We've been burned."

"I've been burned before too," I said.

Amelia frowned. "And you didn't see it coming then either, did you?"

"We never do," Camille said with a sigh. "We never see it coming."

I shook my head. "Can we drop this, please?"

"Look, I'm sure we're wrong," Amelia said. "Just keep both eyes open. That's all I'm saying."

"That's all we're saying," Camille said.

"I'm going back to the unit," I said, standing.

"Can I have your yogurt?" Camille asked.

---

I once heard a psychologist on a radio show say that the level of anger we feel from an accusation or criticism is the exact same level of our belief in the accusation or criticism's truth. No one gets mad if you call them a giraffe, because it's absurd. But if you call them stupid or fat, that's a gut check of their own insecurities.

I guess Amelia and Camille were right. I was angry at them, not because they were making ridiculous accusations but because in the deepest corners of my mind I feared they were right.

What did I really know about Justin, other than he left town every weekend? For all I knew, he had another wife or girlfriend somewhere. Even though I tried to push the thought out of my mind, I was a product of abandonment, and what they said had definitely triggered my deepest insecurities. Maybe I was just an idiot. I certainly hadn't seen who James was until it was too late.

Newton's third law of motion—for every action, there is an equal and opposite reaction—applies to matters of the heart as well as physics. I had felt almost blissful when I came into work that morning, and now my pain was as strong as my happiness had been. The rest of my shift was miserable. Around three, Justin texted to see if we were still on for tonight. All weekend long I had looked forward to being with him, and now I was just anxious and scared. Every time I thought of how happy I'd been, one of my father's sayings went through my head: *If it seems too good to be true, it probably is.* Justin would have answers, right?

I muddled through the rest of my shift, then, without saying goodbye to anyone, walked out into the heavy snowfall to my car.

A snowplow with its flashing yellow lights drove past me, the angry roar of its blade scraping against the asphalt sounding like I felt.

It had snowed nearly two feet while I'd been working, covering everything around me in cold and leaving the parking lot looking like a subdivision of igloos. It took me almost ten minutes to find my car. I could barely open the iced-over door to get out my snowbrush-scraper. I scraped the snow from my windows and hood, then tossed the brush into the back seat of my car and drove home to face the truth.

# CHAPTER

*thirteen*

*Even an open book needs to be read to be appreciated.*

—*Richelle Bach's Diary*

On the drive home the streets were nearly deserted, the way the Salt Lake roads always are in a heavy snowfall. I passed two police cars, a UPS truck, and a fleet of snowplows. The only ones out were those who had to be.

As I pulled up my street I could see, in the light of a streetlamp, the silhouette of someone in my driveway shoveling snow. It was Justin, of course. I should have been grateful, but in the state I was in I just felt more upset.

He looked up at me and waved, then stepped out of the driveway so I could drive in. I pulled my car into the garage.

He walked over to me as I got out of my car. I tried to act normal. "You look like a snowman," I said.

"It's been snowing."

"Yeah, I noticed. Thank you for shoveling my drive."

"My pleasure. How was work?"

"It was okay," I lied. I unlocked the side door to my house, then stepped inside. Justin brushed the snow off his shoulders, kicked the snow from his boots, and followed me in.

"I still need to do your front walk," he said, closing the door behind him.

"It's okay. No one ever uses it, except solicitors."

"Yeah, I saw your sign."

I had posted a handwritten sign on my door that read:

No Solicitors. Really.
Let's not make this awkward.

"I put that up last summer. I was getting way too many door-to-door solicitors. I have a policy that I don't answer the door if I don't know who it is."

"That explains . . ." He stopped.

"That explains what?"

"That's a good policy," he said. "Being a single woman, living alone, it's not smart to open the door to a stranger."

*Kind of what Camille and Amelia were saying.* I took off my coat and hung it in the hall closet.

"You don't seem very happy to see me," Justin said.

*That was certainly direct.* "It's nothing. Everything's fine."

"Fine?" He stepped closer to me. "What is it, Richelle?"

I hesistated a moment, then exhaled. "It's just some of my coworkers."

"What did they do?"

"Nothing. I mean"—I turned to him—"they just asked about you."

He looked intrigued. "They asked about me?" He took off his coat and shoes. "Let's go sit in the living room."

We sat down on opposite ends of the couch. "What did they want to know?"

"Just questions. But I couldn't answer any of them. I felt stupid."

"What kind of questions?"

"Like, are you really a rocket scientist, and what are you doing in Utah if you are? Where do you live? Where do you go on the weekends?" The last question was mine.

To my surprise, he wasn't angry or defensive. He said, "They're fair questions." Suddenly his look of sincerity changed to one of amusement. "They really asked if I was a rocket scientist?"

"Are you?"

He laughed. "Yeah, it does sound a little contrived."

"*Sketchy* was their word."

"Sketchy," he repeated. "I've never been called that before. That's kind of funny." He took out his wallet and extracted a plastic identification card with a NASA hologram and a magnetic strip across the back.

"If we had the right equipment, we could do a biometric retinal scan. That's what they require for entry at the lab, but this might do." He handed the card to me. "That's my NASA ID. I think the photo's a decent enough likeness of me. I could also put you in touch with Shanice in HR; she could verify my employment.

"As for the 'what is a rocket scientist doing in Utah' question, there are probably more than a thousand aerospace engineers in Utah, mostly with aerospace part manufacturers. With my experience, I could land a job at any of them."

I looked down at the card in my hand. It was obviously the real thing.

"We don't actually call ourselves *rocket scientists;* that's more of a cultural thing. I'm an aerospace engineer. I work in the Jet Propulsion Lab, primarily with the 6U CubeSat—it's the spacecraft involved in the Mars Cube One mission we launched last year. It's a communications relay experiment. But then, I suppose if I were really trying to fool you, I could have just looked all that up. You can find it online." He looked into my eyes. "If I made all that up to impress you, you really should be flattered."

I felt embarrassed. I handed him back his card. "I'm sorry. I don't know what to say."

"You don't have to say anything. I get it. Things have moved really fast between us. We've talked about deep things and just kind of skipped over the simple ones. Would it help if I just laid things out for you?"

I wiped my eyes and nodded. "Yes, please."

"Up until last summer I lived in Monrovia, California, with my wife. Monrovia was nice; it was close to my work. I was paid well. We had a Trader Joe's nearby."

I almost smiled.

"Things were great. Until they weren't. Losing my wife wasn't something I saw coming." His voice fell. "I was so affected by it that it was impacting my work. Finally, my boss gave me an ultimatum: I could take a leave of absence or be let go. He said I needed time to heal or counseling, probably both, to get my head back in the game. So I took the leave. I had no reason to stay in California, so I went to Texas to be with my parents. That's where I go on the weekends.

"I came to Utah to see if this was where I wanted to start my life again. My wife always wanted to move here." He looked up at me. "While I'm here, I'm staying at the Crystal Inn off the 215 freeway. I know all this might not make a lot of sense to you, but a lot of things in my life don't make sense right now. I just never expected to be single at this time in my life."

"Why did you come to our writers group? How did you learn about us?"

"It was my wife who told me about it. She knew someone who was in it."

"Who?"

He looked uncomfortable with the question. "I'd rather not say. They don't know who I am. If they knew, it might be a little awkward for them."

"Was it Marjorie?"

He shook his head. "No."

I steeled myself for the question I most wanted answered. "Is there another woman in your life?"

This was the only question I asked that was met with silence. He looked sad or maybe angry that I had asked. Finally, he said, "No, Richelle. I just lost the only woman I've ever loved." He looked at me for a moment, then said, "I haven't told you everything. There are things that are still too painful for me to share—things I'm just not ready to share. Nothing . . . sketchy," he said, grinning slightly. "But I suspect there are things you haven't told me either."

We both sat there for a moment, then he said, "If you want me to leave . . ."

"No," I said. "I don't want you to leave."

"Good. Because being with you is the first time I've felt happy since . . ." He exhaled. "Since I lost her." His eyes showed his emotion. "I know you've been hurt. But as difficult as it is for you, I need you to trust that I care about you and that, when the time is right, I'll tell you everything." He breathed out. "Trust is something that's built over time, but it takes faith to make that leap. If this is going to work, it's going to take some faith."

"Faith in what?" I asked.

"Faith that I won't abandon you."

I thought for a moment, then said, "I can believe that."

He breathed out in relief. "Good. Then may I kiss you now?"

I smiled, even more relieved than he was. "I wish you would."

In the midst of a passionate kiss he suddenly leaned back. His eyes danced. "Sketchy? Really?"

I laughed. "I'm so sorry."

We resumed kissing. After we parted, I said, "Would you like a drink? I have eggnog in the fridge."

"You have eggnog?"

"I bought some. For you."

"I would love an eggnog."

"I don't have any rum, but I have 7Up."

"Close enough," he said.

I went to the kitchen and poured us both a glass, added soda, then brought the glasses out.

Justin took the glass from me and took a sip.

"How is it?" I asked.

"Delicious. It's been a whole year since I had eggnog. Thank you."

"I'm glad you like it." I took a drink myself, then set my glass down. "Would you like to spend Thanksgiving together?"

"I thought you had to work."

"I did. But this morning, before I freaked out, I got the day off."

"I wish I'd known. I made a commitment to spend it with my parents. My sister and her family are flying in just because I'm going to be there. I'm really sorry."

My heart fell. "It's okay. I mean, I should have asked sooner."

Suddenly his expression lightened. "There's no law that says we have to celebrate Thanksgiving on Thursday."

"Actually, I think it is a law," I said. "It's a legal holiday."

He smiled. "Then we'll be scofflaws and celebrate on Tuesday. Just the two of us. Of course, that would mean that we'd have to miss writers group."

"Let me think about that," I said. "Yeah, I could do that."

"Splendid."

"I'm scheduled to work on Tuesday," I said. "But I'm certain I

won't have any problem swapping someone for Thanksgiving."
I felt happy again. "I'm sorry I doubted you."

"You've had your share of betrayals, Richelle. I get it."

"We're two broken people, aren't we?"

He nodded. "That's okay. Broken things usually fit better
together."

# CHAPTER

*fourteen*

*Tonight, Justin and I planned our private Thanksgiving celebration.*
*I like the way this man thinks. Pie in the morning. Pie at night.*
*Sometimes I feel like I've been delaying dessert my whole life.*

*—Richelle Bach's diary*

I t was still snowing when we went out for dinner at a small café less than a mile from my home. We were the only customers in the place. As we were finishing up, our waitress, who was also the café's owner, told us she was closing early to hurry us up. We took a piece of pecan pie and cappuccinos to go and came back to my place to plan our Thanksgiving.

"How do you celebrate Thanksgiving?" I asked.

"Pretty much like everyone else. Except for one excellent addition. We have pie for breakfast."

"Pie is what you're supposed to have after the meal."

"See, that's where people get it wrong. They wait until they're so full they can barely enjoy it. There is nothing better than pumpkin pie and coffee for breakfast to start the day. It's almost as good as cold pizza leftovers."

"You like cold pizza?"

"The next morning? That's when it's the best. And, of course, we still have pie after the meal."

"Is that a Swedish thing?"

"No, it's an Ek family thing. Sweden doesn't do Thanksgiving. Remember, Thanksgiving was about the Pilgrims and Plymouth Rock. They were giving thanks after leaving the religious persecution of England. Sweden back then was doing its own thing, becoming a world power under Gustavus Adolphus the Great."

"So your family just does the American thing?"

"Well, we lived in Alabama, so we did the *southern* American thing. There are three things southerners do better than anyone else."

"What's that?"

"Blues, honky-tonk, and cook. Especially at Thanksgiving. Herb-roasted turkey, baked ham with molasses, and honey sauce; candied sweet potato casserole; baked macaroni and cheese; cornbread dressing; garlic herb mashed potatoes; buttermilk biscuits . . ."

"I want all of that," I said. "Let's have a southern Thanksgiving."

"I'll ask my mother for her recipes."

"Do you have any nonfood traditions?"

"A few. Just before we eat, each of us stands up and says one thing we're grateful for. Then, before we leave the dinner table, we write a thank-you note to someone."

I thought about this for a moment, then asked, "Who did you write the thank-you note to last Thanksgiving?"

He hesitated. "The same person I've written it to for the last five years. My wife."

———————

We started making a Thanksgiving grocery list, then realized it was pointless until we got his mother's recipes, so instead we went out to the couch and watched television with the lights out. Justin laid his head in my lap while I played with his hair. It was idyllic. The snow was still falling outside, isolating us from the rest of the world. Everything felt peaceful and lovely, a far cry from the state I had been in earlier in the day.

Because the storm was unrelenting, I invited him to stay. I put him in Michelle's old room. I got up in the night and went and got in bed with him. I just wanted to be held by him.

CHAPTER

*fifteen*

*I don't know if I believe in ghosts and tales of hauntings, but is it possible that a room can hold the energy of its former occupant? There are times when I think I can feel Michelle's energy in her room. Or maybe it's just the memories. Then again, maybe they're the same thing.*

*—Richelle Bach's diary*

## THURSDAY, NOVEMBER 21

The next morning I woke alone. I rubbed my eyes, then sat up in bed. "Justin?"

No reply. My heart fell. *He must have gone home,* I thought. I looked around the room and couldn't see any of his things. I had no idea what time it was, except that it was later than I usually got up since the blinds glowed from the sun. Even on my days off it was usually dark when I got up. I looked over to my clock then, not seeing it, remembered I was in Michelle's room.

Michelle's room wasn't a room I used, or even went in.

Part of me just wanted to board it up. I don't know why I told Justin to sleep in it. Maybe because I wasn't ready for him to sleep in my father's bed. Or maybe it was just late, and I had just pointed him to the closest room.

I had had the opal dream again. Only this time, Justin was with me. He got down on his knees with me and helped me look for the gems. We still didn't find them.

There was nothing of Justin's in the room, but there was still ample evidence of my sister. The room was preserved from our teen years like a time capsule. The closet was still filled with her high school clothes, and there were two concert posters on the wall, Duran Duran and a "Bohemian Rhapsody" Queen poster.

Across from the bed was Michelle's white dresser with molded panels and brushed brass knobs. Besides dust, there were two things on the dresser: a rose-colored ceramic table lamp and a four-by-six photograph set in a Splash Mountain picture frame from Disneyland with Michelle and me sitting together in the log flume. It's the photo they take just as you start the ride's final plunge.

The picture is telling. I'm holding on to the bars at the sides of the log, my eyes closed, my mouth open, screaming with terror. Michelle is sitting in front of me. She has both eyes open and her hands in the air. She's laughing, thrilled at the sudden fall. The picture summed us up too perfectly. I walked over and turned it on its face.

I went to the window and pulled up the blinds, letting a blinding flash of sunlight into the room. The storm had finally stopped, leaving behind a heavy layer of crystalline snow, crisp against a brilliant blue sky.

I walked out of the room.

"Justin?"

The grandmother clock in the hallway read nearly ten o'clock. I couldn't remember the last time I had slept in that late. The aroma of coffee wafted from the kitchen.

"Justin?"

I heard the sound of a snow shovel scraping the driveway. I looked out the front window. Justin was outside, again clearing the snow from my driveway. The banks on the side of the driveway were more than three feet high. I smiled. He was still here.

I walked back to the kitchen and poured myself a cup of coffee, added milk, then walked back to the front room and opened the door. The cold air braced me.

"You missed a spot," I said.

Justin looked over at me and smiled. "I'd ask how you slept, but I already know."

"Because I was in your bed?"

"Because I didn't sleep well."

"Did I snore? Please don't tell me if I did."

"No, it's not that. It's just . . . you're beautiful."

"Come in. It's cold out."

"Antarctica is cold," he said. "This is more like one of Jupiter's moons."

"Spoken like a rocket scientist."

"Spoken like someone from California. I'm just about done. I'll be in in a moment."

"Would you like some breakfast? I could make an omelet and biscuits."

"That sounds good."

"Okay. Don't be too long."

The biscuits were almost done baking and I was folding the omelet when Justin walked in.

"I don't know why anyone would live where there's snow," he said.

"There's snow in Sweden. A lot of it."

"Probably why my people migrated. Don't people around here have snow removal machines?"

"They're called snow blowers. And I have one."

"You didn't think to tell me this?"

"Sorry. I don't know how to start it. It was my father's. Come, sit down. Your breakfast is ready." I brought the omelet over and set it down in front of him next to a fresh cup of coffee. Then I went back into the kitchen and took the biscuits from the oven. "Would you like butter and honey on your biscuits?"

"Do you have any fruit spread?" he asked.

"You're such a Californian. Normal people call it jam. I have apricot and raspberry."

"Apricot, please."

I brought over the biscuits. "May I butter it for you?"

"Yes, thank you." He watched me as I buttered the biscuit. "You're a pleaser, aren't you?"

"You're the one who keeps shoveling my driveway." I opened the jar of jam, spooned some on the biscuit, and handed it to him. "What if I am? Is that a bad thing?"

"That depends on whether or not you're happy being a pleaser."

"I'm happy pleasing you," I said.

"Me too." A moment later he said, "My mother sent over the recipes this morning. She took pictures of them on her phone and texted them."

"How many did she send?"

"I think six. Here." He handed me his phone.

"It's locked," I said.

"It's seven-seven-seven-seven."

"That's like the most worthless passcode ever."

"One-one-one-one is the most worthless passcode ever, and it doesn't matter. I always have my phone with me. Otherwise, I suffer from *nomophobia*."

"You remembered. I'm impressed." I looked over the recipes. There was turkey, baked ham, candied sweet potato casserole, cornbread dressing, garlic mashed potatoes, buttermilk biscuits, and cheese grits. I texted them to my phone.

"I hope I can find grits. They're not something people in Utah eat."

"I can bring some from Texas," Justin said. "And I'll pick up the pie."

"The pie we're having for breakfast?"

"Our breakfast pie," he said.

With the weather as it was, we spent the rest of the day inside talking, playing cards, and planning our Thanksgiving.

That evening, *It's a Wonderful Life* was playing on cable, so I made a batch of caramel corn and we cuddled on the couch and watched.

"That Donna Reed is one low-maintenance woman," Justin said.

"Just like me," I said.

Justin burst out laughing. I don't think he meant to. He couldn't help it.

I don't remember ever being so happy.

# CHAPTER

## *sixteen*

*Tonight, Justin and I talked about love. He might have given me
the most beautiful definition of the phenomenon I've ever heard.
More than anything, I want to love and to be loved like that.*

*—Richelle Bach's diary*

With Justin gone, I picked up shifts on Friday, Saturday, and Sunday as part of my holiday schedule bargaining. It also helped the time go faster when he was gone.

Justin arrived back in Salt Lake Monday afternoon. I had offered to pick him up at the airport but he declined as he said he needed a car. I'm not sure why since we spent all our time together anyway, but I didn't question him.

We rechecked our Thanksgiving shopping list, then went to the grocery store to fill it. The store was insanely crowded with people preparing for the holiday, and our shopping took nearly two hours. I never found grits, which in the western part of the US are about as foreign as haggis or Marmite. Fortunately, Justin had brought that box from Texas.

We got back home and started preparing for our Thanksgiving supper. There was a lot to be done. I started making the candied sweet potatoes while Justin assembled the rub for the turkey, which was now thawing in the refrigerator. Then I put the cornbread for the stuffing in the oven to bake.

"Are you getting hungry?" I asked.

"As usual."

"Does chili and cornbread sound good?"

"That sounds great."

I heated a can of chili over the stove. When the cornbread was done baking, I cut three slices for us and put the rest aside to dry overnight. I served the bread with bowls of chili and whipped honey butter.

After we'd sat down at the table to eat, Justin said, "I almost forgot—I brought you something." He retrieved a small canvas tote from the living room and set it down on the table next to him. "For you," he said. He took out a mousepad with the NASA logo and the words

## I NEED MY SPACE.

I laughed. "That's funny," I said. "And true."

The second thing he brought from the tote was a metal-framed photograph of him standing next to a man wearing a blue NASA flight jacket. The picture was autographed to Justin.

"Who's that?"

"That's me," he said flippantly.

I grinned. "Yeah, I figured that part out. Who's the guy you're standing next to?"

"That's astronaut Chris Ferguson. He was the commander of the space shuttle *Atlantis*. He flew the very last shuttle flight."

"When did you meet him?"

"We had this meet-and-greet in Pasadena a few years ago. It was kind of a 'thank the little people behind the scenes' thing. He shared a couple of interesting facts with us. He said that the last shuttle mission had a smaller crew than usual, because there was no backup shuttle in case something happened. Their contingency plan, in case they got stuck in space, was to move to the International Space Station and then hitch rides back on the Russian capsules."

"They were going to hitch rides back to Earth?"

He nodded. "That was the escape plan. It was a little more complicated than just sticking out their thumbs. They had to carry their own Russian space suits, which cost more than ten million dollars apiece.

"The other thing he told us was that the Apollo 11 astronauts Neil Armstrong and Buzz Aldrin had to go through customs after returning from the moon. They declared their moon rocks as souvenirs and listed their travel route as embarking from Cape Canaveral with a brief layover on the moon."

"That's a joke, right?"

"It's a joke, but it's true. That's bureaucracy for you."

I lifted the picture of Justin. "Thank you. This is a good picture of you."

"I thought you might like some more evidence."

"I don't need any more evidence. But I like having a picture of you." I folded out the stand and placed the picture upright on the table. "I'm going to keep it on my nightstand. That way, you'll be the last person I see when I go to bed and the first I see when I wake up."

A warm smile crossed his face. "I like that. Of course, the real thing would be better."

I smiled. "That would be better."

We finished our dinner, then I poured a couple of glasses of white wine and we took them out to my sofa. Sitting down, I said, "I thought we should toast our anniversary."

"Our anniversary?"

"It's been two weeks."

Justin looked surprised. "It's really only been two weeks?"

"Just two weeks ago, you wandered haplessly into our Calliope meeting."

"Two weeks," he said. "I feel like I've known you my whole life."

I liked that. "Me too," I said. We were both quiet a moment; then I said, "Do you believe in love at first sight?"

He looked at me thoughtfully. "I guess that depends on what you mean by love. If you mean romantic love—that animal, chemical attraction—absolutely I do. I felt that way the first time I saw you." He smiled. "It's the ignition switch on the rocket engines.

"But it's not real love," he said. "At least, it's not how I think of it."

"Oh? And how do you think of love?"

He lowered his glass to his lap. "Love is like a rose. It's the beautiful, elegant petals and perfume that sell the flower. But those things don't last very long. The petals wilt and die. In the end, it's the stem—the thorny, sturdy green stem—that keeps the flower alive. It's what endures after the petals wilt and the perfume fades.

"Love is two old people doing crossword puzzles together at the end of their lives and helping each other when they become too feeble to walk. It might not sound exciting, but it's better than that. It's love."

I don't know why, but my eyes welled up. "That's beautiful." I lifted my glass. "To stems."

He lifted his and we toasted. "To stems."

It was a beautiful start to our private Thanksgiving celebration.

# CHAPTER

## *seventeen*

*I finally told Justin about the recurring dream I've been having. I felt like Pharaoh asking Joseph to interpret his dream. I didn't especially like his interpretation—not because I didn't agree with it but more likely because I did.*

—Richelle Bach's diary

## TUESDAY, NOVEMBER 26
## (FAUX THANKSGIVING)

I got up early and went to the gym in anticipation of the day's gluttony. Ever since I'd joined, the gym had been insanely crowded on Thanksgiving morning, so I was baffled as to why there were so few people there. I had forgotten it was only Thanksgiving for Justin and me.

I went home and showered, then put on something I hadn't worn in a while, a form-fitting green sweater dress with a brown, braided leather waist belt with matching thigh boots.

I didn't get to dress up much, and I thought I looked cute. I hoped Justin did too.

I put on one of my father's albums, the Carpenters' *Christmas Portrait*. As I put some coffee on, I got a little sentimental hearing Karen Carpenter sing "I'll Be Home for Christmas." It was one of my father's holiday favorites. For the first time in my life, he wouldn't be home for Christmas.

In my typical efficient manner, I had printed off all of Justin's mom's recipes and stacked them in order like I did at the hospital with patient assignments.

*Herb-roasted turkey*
*Baked ham*
*Candied sweet potato casserole*
*Cornbread dressing*
*Garlic mashed potatoes*
*Buttermilk biscuits*
*Cheese grits*

I had made two last-minutes changes to the menu, something my father would have called an audible. For the football illiterate, that's when a quarterback makes a change to the play after they're already lined up. (For reasons still unknown, my father thought it important that Michelle and I know football terminology.)

I picked up a precooked ham. There was a real advantage to celebrating Thanksgiving before the actual holiday, as one Thanksgiving I stood outside the honey-baked ham store for nearly an hour.

I also substituted my favorite Parker House rolls for the buttermilk biscuits and added a salad with candied pecans, strawberries, and feta cheese with a strawberry vinaigrette.

The Carpenters album had finished and Mitch Miller and the Gang were singing "Sleigh Ride" when Justin arrived. I took the pan off the stove, then went and opened the door for him. Justin was carrying a paper sack with the name of a nearby bakery I loved.

"Happy Thanksgiving," I said.

"Happy Thanksgiving." We kissed.

"You know you don't have to ring the doorbell. You can just walk in."

"I tried. Your door was locked." He kicked the slush from his shoes, then stepped inside. Outside it was cloudy, but not snowing for once. At least for now. The weather report I watched at the gym said it was supposed to start snowing late afternoon and continue off and on through Thanksgiving. I shut the door behind him.

"What is that divine smell?" he asked, walking toward the kitchen.

"It's your mom's cornbread stuffing recipe. I was just making the herb butter. Sage, thyme, parsley, and rosemary."

"It smells like my childhood," he said.

"Your childhood smells like herb butter?"

He grinned. "Pretty much." He set the bag he was carrying on the counter. "I brought breakfast." He lifted a box from the bag and set it on the counter, then took a pie from the box. It was artfully decorated with rosette-shaped dollops of whipped cream.

"That's a really fancy pie."

"Nothing but the best for our Thanksgiving. I got it from that bakery you like. How big a piece do you want?"

"Culturally, I'm obligated to say small, but I reserve the right to seconds."

"You got it. Where do you keep your pie plates?"

"That cupboard there," I said, pointing. "There's a pie server in that second drawer."

Justin found the plates and server then cut the pie.

"Breakfast is served," he said, carrying two plates to the table.

"I'll be right over. I just need to finish the stuffing. I made coffee."

"I'll get it." He poured two cups of coffee, added milk to mine, then brought them to the table as well. "That is a big turkey," he said.

"It's the smallest they had, but it's still way too much for just us."

"Don't they have smaller turkeys?"

"Yes. They're called chickens."

He laughed. "It's just as well. You can never have too much Thanksgiving turkey. The bird's just so versatile. You can make turkey sandwiches, turkey noodle soup, turkey tetrazzini, turkey lasagna . . ."

"I'm pretty sure you just made that last one up."

"No. It's legit."

"And don't forget we have ham. So, unless you take leftovers back with you, I'm going to be eating Thanksgiving for the next two weeks."

"I don't think ham and gravy will travel well in my suitcase."

I set the saucepan on one of the unlit back burners, then went and sat down next to Justin at the table. I first took a small bite of whipped cream, then a large bite of pie. "Mmm. I like your tradition."

"You're welcome to it," he said. "So what comes after the stuffing?"

"The rolls still have another half hour to rise, and we need to mash the potatoes. Do you mind peeling the potatoes? There's only four."

"Just put me to work."

We finished our coffee and pie, then went back to the kitchen. Justin brought the potatoes from the pantry and stood at the sink to wash and peel them.

While we were cooking Justin asked, "How's work going?"

"It's good."

"It must be. You keep going back."

"I like helping the kiddos. Two weeks ago, I had a five-year-old boy with leukemia. Even though the rooms are never really that dark, he was so afraid of monsters that he wouldn't let his mother leave. You could see that she was past exhausted. Then I had an idea. I called the pharmacy and had them fill a spray bottle with water and print a label that read Monster Spray. Spray Room Before Bed. Repeat if Necessary. 1 Refill.

"The pharmacy sent up the bottle and I showed it to the little boy, then I sprayed all around his room. Then I gave him the bottle and said, 'This stuff always works. Guaranteed. Monsters won't come within a mile of it. It turns them to glue.'

"The little boy was so excited. He said, 'Cool. Maybe one will come and I can spray it.' I said, 'Maybe we'll get lucky, but probably not. I've never seen a monster once I've sprayed this stuff. Sometimes they don't come around for weeks.' The mother blew me a kiss and went home. She was so grateful."

Justin was smiling. "You're good to those children."

"I care about them. I don't have my own, so I guess I borrow them for a little while." I looked at him. "It's either that or become a cat lady."

"You made a wise choice." He stood back from the sink. "The potatoes are done. Now what?"

"You can set the table. The china's in that cabinet. The silver is in the bottom drawer."

"On it."

As he set the table I said, "Have I ever told you about the dreams I keep having over and over?"

"You're having a recurring dream?"

"I've had it at least twice a week for the last four or five months. Only you were in it last time."

"I made your dream? Tell me about it."

"In this dream, I'm standing in a big field. I'm holding two opals in my hand when they suddenly get really hot and I drop them in the grass. I panic but I can't find them."

"Like the opal you're wearing?"

"I think it's the same one. What do you think it means?"

"I've heard that a recurring dream means your subconscious is trying to tell you something you don't want to admit with your waking mind."

"I have no idea what that would be."

"So let's analyze it. What does your opal symbolize to you?" He glanced at my pendant. "It must be important to you, since you're always wearing it."

"Well, it's a precious stone, so it's worth a lot of money. It's also precious because it was a gift from my father."

"So why are there two opals in your dream? Why not just yours?"

"Like I told you, my father bought two opals—one for Michelle and one for me."

". . . And you dropped both of them," he said. "When did you start having these dreams?"

"About four months ago."

"Not long after Michelle died."

I hadn't thought of that. "What if it means that in losing my sister, I also lost myself?" I looked at him. "Do you think I'm lost?"

"Do you feel lost?"

"Sometimes."

"It's worth considering." He hesitated a moment, then said, "You got an expensive opal for high school graduation, and I got a graduation card and ten dollars."

"Ten dollars?"

"Honestly, I think my parents forgot to get me something, and it's what my father had in his wallet. They're great parents, but they're not really sentimental. There was one exception. When I graduated from Caltech my parents came out to see me walk. My father brought a bottle of Pappy Van Winkle to toast my success. Just the two of us. I mean, it was a nice gesture."

"What's Pappy Van Winkle?"

"It's a brand of bourbon. It costs about $125 a bottle, but some bars will charge that much for a single shot. Some of it sells for as much as thirty thousand dollars a bottle."

"Why is it so expensive?"

"Because it's made from unobtainium."

I looked at him blankly. "What's that?"

"It's a pun," he said. "It means it's hard to get."

"Un-obtain-ium. Got it." I put the turkey in the oven then said, "I'd like to meet your parents."

"They're looking forward to meeting you."

I turned back to him. "You've told them about me?"

"Of course."

I turned back and smiled.

# CHAPTER

*eighteen*

*What a beautiful day it was. You know it's a good Thanksgiving when your heart is as full as your stomach.*

—Richelle Bach's diary

We were finishing up cooking our meal when Justin asked, "How's your book coming?"

"Which one?"

"Which one are you working on?"

"You mean which one am I *not* working on. I haven't written a word in weeks."

"You've got writer's block?"

"Is that what you call yourself?"

He grinned. "So now it's my fault?"

"Well, I was making progress until you came around. So who else would I blame?"

"Do you have to blame someone else for what you don't do?"

"Of course. That's what authors do. Truthfully, if I spent half as much time writing my book as I do worrying about not writing my book, I'd have written a tome by now."

"Is that true for all writers?"

"Maybe. Every writer I know has a love-hate relationship with their book. Except for Fred. He's just in love with his book. He loves it so much he's written it six times."

Justin smiled. "What is it about being a writer that appeals to you?"

"I've just always loved books. There's something magical about them, the ability to create feelings from ink on a page. Really, it's a form of alchemy."

"I like that," he said.

"In college I had a dual major—biology and English literature. In my heart of hearts, I wanted to be a novelist, but that's not the kind of thing you stake a career on, you know?"

"Why is that?"

"To begin with, there are like a million new books a year. Only a few of them ever sell enough for the writer to make a living from it."

"I don't think it's the financial aspect you're most interested in," he said.

"What do you think it is?"

"I think it's the idea of leaving a legacy. I think we all hope that something we did on this earth will outlive us."

"That won't happen with me."

"It already has. Those children whose lives you saved. And then you have all their future children. You already have a legacy. Your impact is far greater than you know."

"Well, it's a team effort."

"Of course; most of the time, it's a team. But teams are made up of individuals. Still, I'd bet you've saved at least one life by something you alone did."

I thought about it. "Twice that I know of. Once a doctor misdiagnosed a patient. The doctor said if I hadn't caught it, we would have lost him. Another time a patient was given the wrong medication."

"*Voilà*—your legacy," he said.

He had no idea how much that meant to me.

━━━━━━

While Justin carved the turkey, I got the rolls out of the oven and we sat down to eat.

"Before we eat I'd like to say a prayer," I said.

"Please."

I took Justin's hand and we bowed our heads. "Dear God, thank you for all that we have, the abundance of our lives. We pray for the souls of all those we're missing at this time. And I'm grateful for my friend, Justin, and for his kindness and patience with me. Amen."

"Amen," he said. He looked at me. "Thank you."

"One more thing before we eat. Can we do your tradition? You know, say one thing we're grateful for."

"You just did," he said. "But of course. Would you mind if I went first?"

"Of course not."

He looked down for a moment, then back up at me. "This Thanksgiving I'm most grateful that you let me into your life. I'm grateful for every minute we've spent together, and I'm grateful for the hope that those minutes might turn into years. That's all."

My heart was full. "Thank you. So do I." I took a moment to gather my thoughts. "Okay, my turn. I was so afraid of what this Thanksgiving would be like. I had no one in my life to spend it with." My eyes started to well up. "This Thanksgiving, I'm mostly grateful that I have someone to be grateful for." I looked into his eyes. "That I have you to be grateful for."

He lifted his water glass. "To us."

"To us," I said back.

We started eating. The amount of food on the table was excessive. We could have fed a large family.

"That's a lot of food," I said.

Justin nodded. "This is a ridiculously large amount of food. It's too bad we don't have more people here to share it."

"I wish my family were here to share it." A wave of nostalgia passed through me. "I miss them. I miss the way it used to be when I was young, sitting down at the same table. Just the three of us." A sad smile crossed my face. "My father used to call us the Three Amigos. I never thought that one day it would just be me."

Justin's demeanor became more serious. "Do you think you'll ever be with your father and sister again?"

"You mean in some kind of afterlife?"

He nodded.

"I don't know about the whole heaven and hell thing, but I'm pretty certain there's a consciousness after death."

"Why is that?"

"Because of an experience I had at work."

"Tell me about it."

I set down my fork. "It was my third year in the PICU. I

had an eleven-year-old girl with rheumatic heart disease. During her care she coded. She was gone for six minutes before we revived her. You can imagine how intense that is. I was preparing an IV syringe and I dropped it on the ground and had to get a second one. I remember I said a prayer for her in my mind. It was a simple one; I just said, 'God, don't let this sweet child die.' We were lucky. She didn't.

"The next day I was walking outside her door when she called to me. I went inside her room. She was covered in lines and IVs, but she was sitting up in bed. I asked, 'How are you feeling?' She said, 'You were there when I died.' That's not something we talk about with children, so I asked, 'Who told you you died?' She said, 'No one. I was there.' Then she said, 'I saw you. You dropped a shot.' I knew for a fact that she was flatlined at that time. I asked her how she knew that. Again she said, 'I saw you. You asked God to not let me die.' I said, 'I only said that in my mind. How did you hear me?' She said, 'You can hear what people think when you leave your body.'

"Then she asked, 'Is Spider-Man going to come back? I wanted to see him.' I said, 'You saw Spider-Man?' She said, 'Yes. I want to see him when he comes back.'

"That kind of made me doubt everything, like it was all just a fantasy she was having. Later that afternoon I was going over my educational modules with my charge nurse when she said, 'Did you see Spider-Man yesterday?' I said, 'Spider-Man?' She said, 'Yeah, it's great. He came by the PICU yesterday to see if he could visit the children. He's a college student who spent a lot of time in the hospital as a kid and wanted to give back. He had one of those realistic costumes and the physique to pull it off, if you know what I mean. I wouldn't mind getting caught in his web.'

"I asked her what time he was there. She said it was just after she got back from lunch, around one. Maybe a little earlier. She said he was there for about an hour. The little girl had flatlined at four minutes after one.

"That afternoon I went back to the girl and said, 'How did you know Spider-Man was here?' She said, 'I saw him. He was in the hall.' I asked, 'Did you see anything else?' She said, 'I saw the light.' My Sunday School kicked in, and I asked, 'Was someone in the light?' She said, 'No. He *was* the light. He said it wasn't time for me to die.' Then she lay back and closed her eyes. That's all she would say."

We were both quiet for a moment, then Justin said, "Thank you for sharing that."

"I've had other experiences since then. I've also talked with others in the unit who've had similar experiences. It seems intellectually dishonest to dismiss experiences like that."

"If your father and sister were here right now, what would you say to them?"

I thought for a moment, then said, "Eat."

———

We took our time eating. Everything tasted delicious except for the grits, which I'd managed to burn. Justin didn't say a word about it. After dinner Justin asked, "Ready for more pie?"

"If I have one more bite I'll probably explode. If I don't, my scale will. How about later?"

"Later it is."

I folded my napkin and set it on the table. "This was one of the best Thanksgivings ever."

"You're a very good cook," he said.

"I wasn't talking about the food," I said.

Justin looked at me affectionately. "Do you have Christmas off?"

"I'm scheduled to work, but my manager told me she would let me have it off if I asked. I assumed you'd be in Texas with your family."

"I'm planning on it," he said. "I'm hoping you'll come with me."

"You want me to spend Christmas with your family?"

He nodded. "I know it's a big step, but yes, I would. They're all very excited to meet you."

"They?"

"My parents, my brother and sisters. What do you think?"

"I'd love to," I said.

He smiled wide. "I'm excited for you to meet my family."

"Me too," I said. I wasn't sure what else to say. We'd clearly just reached a new place in our relationship. "Well, I better get started cleaning up."

"No," Justin said. "That would be a violation of tradition. After the gluttony, it's time for a nap."

"Let me put some of this in the fridge."

"I'll help you," he said.

A few minutes later we lay down together on the couch. I loved being held by him.

I woke to the sound of dishes clanging in the kitchen. When I walked in, the kitchen was nearly clean. Justin was washing the last of the dishes.

"You didn't wait for me," I said.

"No, I couldn't sleep."

"I'll finish up."

"How about you put things away, since I have no idea where you want them."

"Deal," I said.

We finished the dishes, ate some pie, then went outside for a short walk in the brisk air.

It started snowing again. On the way back to my house I said, "Would you like to spend the night again?"

He didn't answer.

I turned to him. "I didn't mean . . ."

"Okay," he said.

If he had asked me to marry him right then I would have said yes.

# CHAPTER

## *nineteen*

*The most painful events in our lives are usually the things that broadside us when we're worried about something else. It's like getting run over on the sidewalk as we're cautiously preparing to cross the street.*

*—Richelle Bach's diary*

## WEDNESDAY, NOVEMBER 27

I woke the next morning to the sound of the shower running. I looked at my clock. It was already after eight. I was upset that I'd slept in. Justin's flight was in just two and a half hours and, with the holiday crowds, he needed to be at the airport early. I went to the kitchen to make us some coffee.

As I was walking out of my room, I heard the ding from a text message. I knew it was Justin's phone, as mine was still charging on my nightstand. I looked around for his phone but couldn't see it. As I walked past the living room, I heard another ding coming from the couch.

It crossed my mind that it might be a notification from the

airline delaying his flight, which, I admit, I hoped for. I found his phone on the sofa cushion and lifted it. There was a text message.

**OLIVIA**

I miss you

The three words triggered me. I stood there with his phone in my hand, frozen. Then, almost without thinking, I typed in his passcode: 7777. At the top of the screen of texts was the name Olivia. I pushed on it, opening a string of messages over the last two days.

**OLIVIA**

I wish you were here

**OLIVIA**

Why do you keep leaving me?

**OLIVIA**

♥

Numbness spread through my body, just like it had when I'd walked in on James and Michelle. This Olivia had an 817 area code, which I knew from my college days. Fort Worth, Texas. There was another reason Justin was flying to Texas every weekend.

I set his phone back down on the sofa's arm, then went into the kitchen to collect myself. About ten minutes later Justin walked out of the bathroom, drying his hair with a towel. He had pants on but no shirt.

"Good morning, gorgeous. I debated waking you, but I figured you don't get to sleep in that often."

"Thank you," I said softly.

"I'm sorry I've got to leave so early. I have to return the rental car."

"It's okay."

He must have detected the pain in my voice. He put down the towel. "Are you okay?"

I fought to hide the myriad emotions churning inside. I forced a smile. "I'm fine. I'm just sad you're leaving."

"Me too. I wish I could stay."

"I understand. Family calls."

"What should I do with this?" he said, holding out the towel.

"Just leave it in the bathroom. I'll get it."

He walked back to the bathroom. Just a few minutes later he came back out fully dressed and carrying his bag. "You're off next Monday, right?"

I nodded. "Yes."

"Then I'll take the earlier flight back."

"Okay."

I must not have sounded too excited, since he looked at me with a puzzled expression. "You do want me back . . . ?"

"Of course I do."

He still looked puzzled. "Have you seen my phone?"

"It's on the couch."

"Okay." He walked over and picked it up. He glanced down at the screen, then slid the phone in his coat pocket. He turned back to me. "I'd better be on my way. I'll see you next week."

I didn't say anything. He walked over to kiss me, but I turned away. He looked at me with surprise. "Richelle . . ."

"You'd better go," I said. "The airport's going to be busy."

"Are you sure you're okay?"

"I'm fine. I'm always fine."

"All right, I'll call you."

He kissed me on the cheek, then walked out of the house. I walked over and looked out the window as he pulled out of my driveway. Tears streamed down my face. I wished I hadn't taken the day off. Now I had to sit here all day alone in my misery. Why did this keep happening to me? I went into my room, lay facedown on my bed, and cried.

# CHAPTER

*twenty*

*Is this hell, to be stuck in a continual loop of our greatest disappointments?*

*—Richelle Bach's diary*

# THURSDAY, NOVEMBER 28
# (THANKSGIVING DAY)

J ustin texted me as soon as he landed in Texas. I didn't see his text until the next morning, as I had turned my phone off. It beeped with a text the moment I turned it back on.

**JUSTIN**

Happy Thanksgiving.
I'm grateful you are in my life.
I'm so sorry I had to leave yesterday.
I love you.

My aching heart was torn. I wanted to believe him. I also wanted to throw my phone against the wall. I turned it back off, put it in my purse, and drove to work.

A few hours into my shift Amelia approached me in the hall.

"Happy Thanksgiving," she said.

"Is it?" I asked.

"Right? How did you get stuck working today?"

"I traded for it."

She shook her head. "You are a masochist, my friend."

"Apparently."

"I've been meaning to apologize for lunch last week. Camille and I were out of line. We weren't trying to be paranoid, we were just worried about you. I'm sure he's a great guy."

"No, you were right about him," I said. "He wasn't who I thought he was."

Amelia looked upset. "Oh no. I'm so sorry. You've been so happy."

"Life has a way of making us pay for our happiness."

She gave me a hug. "I'm sorry, honey. Do you want to get a drink after work?"

"Thanks, but I better not. I might not stop drinking."

"You don't need tomorrow off, do you? I can cover for you."

*Now she was asking for my shifts.* "No thank you. I need the distraction."

"I really am sorry, Richelle. I was hoping I was wrong about him. If you need anything I'm here."

My dad used to quote a Bible verse: "Sufficient unto the day is the evil thereof." Basically it means we shouldn't worry about the future, since each day already contains enough evil and suffering. That certainly described my life at that time. It was as if a cloud had parked over me.

Near the end of my shift, my little purple-haired friend, Ryan, passed away. I was there when we withdrew care. His mother looked like she was going to pass out. Even though I was off at seven, I sat with her for almost an hour. Before she left, she told me that her other son had taken his life two weeks earlier. I don't know how she was still breathing. People always say that no matter how awful things are, there's always someone suffering more. It's true. It's not really helpful, but it's true.

I didn't turn on my phone until I got home. As soon as I did, it beeped with three messages, all from Justin.

**JUSTIN**

Please call me.

**JUSTIN**

Richelle, what is going on?

The last message was the most direct.

**JUSTIN**

Am I coming on Monday?

I turned my phone off again and went to bed.

# CHAPTER

*twenty-one*

*I found an online support group for twins who've lost twins. They
call themselves "twinless twins." I believe that in the heart of every
twin is the belief that we came in together, so we should go out together—
which, of course, is rarely the case. They say this creates survivor's
guilt. Or do I feel guilt for not feeling guilty? I honestly don't know where
I fit into all this. I lost my twin long before her heart stopped.*

—Richelle Bach's diary

I f you're still with me, I ask that you don't judge me too
harshly. Obviously I have abandonment issues, but at least
I came by them honestly. My mother left me when I was
just three years old. It may be impossible to know the full
impact that had on me, but the pain and fear that caused re-
mains in me, occasionally rising in my heart like groundwater.
James's abandonment only solidified and confirmed fears that
already existed.

My twin, my greatest connection for most of my life, had
abandoned me three times. First to Europe, then to California,
and then, in a final departure, to death.

My father had been the great counterweight to those

feelings. But now, even he had left me. I know it wasn't his choice, but the heart isn't always that rational or forgiving.

I once read a magazine article on why abandonment causes such serious and painful emotion. The article's author, a psychologist from Washington State, claimed it was because the human child is the most vulnerable member among all species. A baby alligator can hunt and defend itself within hours of being born, but to abandon a human baby is to ensure its demise. The article claimed that hardwired into the human psyche is the primal fear that abandonment equals death. Consequently, the heart facing abandonment is literally fighting for its very survival. That's what it felt like to me.

The next few days passed without a word from Justin. It angered me that I still missed him even after what I'd discovered. It's odd, but I've found that the pain of abandonment and the pain of betrayal don't necessarily charge from the same emotional account. That's why a child will still go to a parent for comfort even after being beaten by that parent.

My heart was broken and confused, my emotions spinning like one of those carnival prize wheels. I continually was tempted to respond to one of his messages, either in anger or desperation—depending on the minute—but then I'd remind myself of the texts I'd seen and my heart would harden.

With each passing day my pain grew, numbing my sadness with the anesthesia of anger. Anger at him and anger at myself. I had been a fool to so quickly throw my heart out there, just to have it crushed again.

# CHAPTER

*twenty-two*

*There are two chattering women inside me. One is desperate and lonely, the other angry and afraid. I don't care for either of their company, nor do I trust either of their advice.*

*—Richelle Bach's diary*

## MONDAY, DECEMBER 2

November slipped into December almost without my notice. The holiday season was in full bloom. Even though Christmas music flowed from the hospital's sound systems, I didn't feel it. I even let my colleagues know that I was willing to pick up extra shifts but I got no takers. I guess they were spooked by the ghost of Christmas bills past.

I didn't work on Monday, so I did some laundry, then spent the day working on my PICU book. I had started with the *Prodigal Daughter* book but, considering the mental state I was in, everything I wrote just sounded mean.

Around five that evening my doorbell rang. As usual, I greeted the bell with distrust. I looked out the peephole. It was Justin.

Again, there were two women fighting within me. One wanted to fling open the door and fall into his arms; the other wanted to bar the door until he left. He had rung the doorbell twice and knocked when my two women agreed on a compromise. Leaving the door still chained, I opened it, exposing just half my face.

"What do you want?"

"I don't understand what's going on, Richelle. Why are you acting this way?"

"Guess," I said.

"I honestly have no idea."

He really did look clueless. Watching him standing there in pain, I felt as cruel as I had made him out to be. Then he said, "I love you, Richelle. I'm sorry for . . . whatever." He turned to walk away. At that moment the battle between the two women reached a crescendo. The lonely woman prevailed. I unchained and opened the door. "Justin."

He turned back.

"Let's talk."

Without a word, he walked in and sat down on my couch. I sat in the armchair across from him. He looked vulnerable, like a little boy. I was still conflicted. The maternal part of me wanted to comfort him.

We sat there silently for probably a minute, though it felt much longer. I'm not sure what I was waiting for. In this emotional chess match, it was my move. Finally, I just said it.

"Who's Olivia?"

Justin stared at me. Then he raked his hands through his hair. "That's why you're so upset?"

"Yes."

"I'm guessing you read a text from her." He sighed heavily, laying his head in his hands while I awaited his answer. When he looked up I couldn't tell if he was angry or sad. "Olivia's my daughter."

For a moment I was speechless. "You have a daughter?"

"That's why I have to leave every weekend."

"Your wife left her with you?"

"Yes. That's why I moved to Texas, so my mother could help me with her. I'm the only parent she has."

I could hardly believe it. "How old is she?"

"She's almost six. Going on twenty."

"She can text?"

"Like I said, going on twenty."

My head spun. "Why didn't you just tell me?"

His voice pitched. "Why didn't you . . ." he stopped himself. "I was protecting her. She just lost her mother. She's a pretty fragile little girl." His brow fell. "You could have just asked, Richelle. I would have told you the truth. I was going to tell you about her this visit." He breathed out heavily. "I told you there were things I wasn't ready to tell you. You said you would trust me."

I felt ashamed. "I know. When I saw the text . . . it just triggered something. It was like someone else took over."

He again raked his hands through his hair. "This morning,

I had to force myself to get on the plane to see you. Do you know why I did?"

I shook my head. "I have no idea."

"I told myself that you were worth fighting for." He looked me in the eyes. "Am I?"

At that moment, all the feelings I had had for him flooded back. I got up and walked across the room and sat down next to him. "Yes, you are. Can you please forgive me? Again?"

He pulled my head into his chest. "Yes, I will. If you'll promise to remember I'm on your side."

---

We stayed in the rest of the evening. After the emotional intensity of the past few days it was a relief to do something as mindless as watch television. I even watched an hour of boxing with him. I think it gave Justin a way to release the frustration he must have felt over the last few days.

Before we went to bed I asked, "When will I get to meet Olivia?"

"When you come for Christmas," he said.

"Will you tell me about her?"

At that moment I saw a side of Justin I hadn't seen before. A beautiful but sad smile crossed his face. "She's my life. A couple of weeks ago I enrolled her in fairy camp. They gave her a wand and these little pink tights with wings sewn into them.

"The first day they tossed glitter in her hair and told her that she now had special fairy eyes and could see things no one else could see. The next few days she wouldn't let me wash her hair." His smile slowly vanished. He choked up. "A couple days later she told me that because she was a fairy she could see her mommy whenever she wanted."

His words faded into silence. I wanted to cry for both of them.

# CHAPTER

*twenty-three*

*I've never been the superstitious type. I've never worried about black cats, broken mirrors, or Friday the 13th—though, after today, I'm open to rethinking the latter.*

*—Richelle Bach's diary*

## FRIDAY, DECEMBER 13

We spent the next few days healing our relationship. I had wounded Justin deeply, and all I wanted to do was make it up to him. I had to work Wednesday to Friday, so I invited him to stay at my place in Michelle's old room. The arrangement was perfect, since I wanted to spend every waking moment with him.

Thursday night we did a little Christmas shopping and bought some toys for Olivia, which was easy since she loved all things mermaid and unicorn. We even found a mermaid-unicorn doll.

When Justin asked me what I wanted for Christmas I said, "You."

He said, "How would I wrap that?"

"With as little as possible."

He just smiled.

Every day, I found myself counting down the minutes until work was over, something I had never done before. When Amelia asked me why I was so happy again, I told her that Justin really was who I'd hoped he was.

Friday morning, I got up at my usual time, showered, put on my scrubs, then went into Michelle's room, where Justin was still asleep. He was flying out around noon, and my heart ached in anticipation of his departure. I lay down on the bed next to him. I just looked at him. Savored him. Then I kissed his stubbled face until he woke. "Good morning, love."

"Good morning, gorgeous," he answered, his eyes still not open. "Is it morning?" His voice was raspy and cute.

"It's morning for us worker bees."

"Does that make me a drone?"

"Only if I can be the queen bee."

"That never ends well for the drone," he said. "Death by honeymoon."

"There are worse ways to go," I said.

He smiled.

"It's Friday the thirteenth. Do you think we'll have bad luck?"

He reached over and pulled me onto him. "Does this feel like bad luck?"

"No. I feel very lucky." I lay my head against his chest. "It's still snowing. Do you think they'll cancel your flight?"

"Only if we're lucky," he said. "Do you want me to make you some breakfast?"

"You're sweet. But I'm running late. I'll grab a bagel on the way out." I kissed him, then stood. "Travel safe, okay?"

He sat up. "Are you coming to Texas for Christmas?"

"Yes. I'm asking for the time off today."

He smiled. "Good. I want to book our flights early and save a little money for a change. These last-minute bookings are wreaking havoc on my budget."

"I'm sorry," I said. "Will you be back on Monday?"

"If I can wait that long."

"I can't." I crawled back on the bed and we kissed some more. He again wrapped his arms around me, pulling me tightly into him. After another round of kissing, I tried to push myself away. He just held me tighter. "I've got to go," I said, laughing. "I'm going to be late."

"Can't you just call in sick?"

"No. You're leaving in two hours."

"I know. I think leaving gets more painful each time."

"Excruciating," I said. "But you know what they say, absence makes the heart grow fonder."

"Absence makes the heart grow *fungus*," he said.

I laughed. "You are so weird. Text me when you're home so I know you're safe." We kissed again, then I got off the bed, holding his hand for as long as I could until we parted.

"Don't forget to text me," he said after me. "And be careful on those roads."

"I'm always careful," I said. I walked out of the room, grabbed a bagel, a protein bar, and a bottle of apple juice, then went outside into the brisk twilight winter air. The sun had just begun to clear the mountains, illuminating the crystalline world around me in a shimmering blue-gold. Everything looked stunningly beautiful. Or, maybe, love affects the eyesight.

The plows hadn't kept up with the snow and the drive to the hospital was agonizingly slow. I passed several accidents on the way.

I pulled into the parking lot just a few minutes before my shift and hurried into the hospital, not just because it was snowing but because in six years I had never been late to work and I wanted to keep that record.

When I got to the unit I was met by Amelia.

"You're here early," I said. Amelia wasn't as punctual as me and more than once had been reprimanded for being tardy.

"It wasn't my choice. I had to take TRAX. Guy's car died last night."

"Now you'll have to find a new boyfriend."

She rolled her eyes.

"Did you see if Terri is here?"

"She's in her office. But I'm warning you, she's a grizzly this morning."

"Oh, really."

"Trust me. You don't want what she's giving."

I walked back and knocked on Terri's door. "Come in." Amelia wasn't wrong. Her voice did sound scary.

I opened the door. "Hi."

Terri looked at me with an unusually pained expression. "I was waiting for you to get in. We need to talk."

"What about?"

"Take a seat," she said. As soon as I was sitting she said, "You go first."

"I've been thinking about what you said a few weeks ago about not working so much and I would like Christmas off after all."

She looked at me for a moment, then exhaled slowly. "Unfortunately, you will."

"Unfortunately?"

Terri didn't blink. "Is there anything you'd like to tell me before I get started?"

Her question felt as threatening as it was cryptic. "No. Is something wrong?"

"Richelle, this is your last chance to come clean."

"Come clean? I honestly have no idea what you're talking about."

She took a deep breath. "Someone in the unit has been diverting opioids. We believe it was you."

My chest froze. "Me? Why would you think that?"

"Two witnesses informed on you. We checked the missing drugs with our employees' work schedules, and it confirmed that you were the only nurse on the unit who was here every time drugs went missing."

"That's because I work more than anyone else."

"That doesn't answer how someone could steal drugs when they're not here. This is a very serious charge, Richelle. There's going to be an investigation."

I couldn't believe what I was hearing. "You don't believe I did that, do you?"

"It doesn't matter what I believe."

I could hardly speak, my chest was so tight. "I don't use drugs. I don't steal. You know I don't break rules. I've never even been late to work."

"People don't always steal drugs for themselves. You know the street value of opioids."

"I don't, Terri. Why would I?" Tears began running down my face. "I don't even need money. My father left me an inheritance. How can you believe this?"

Terri didn't answer for a moment, then said, "Off the record, I don't, Richelle. But the witnesses provided solid evidence. We have to handle this according to protocol. My hands are tied."

"I don't understand. How could there be evidence if I haven't done anything?"

"That's a good question."

"Who are these witnesses?"

"I can't tell you."

"Don't I have a right to face my accusers?"

"Not during the investigation. You will in court."

"In court?" My heart felt like it would stop. I had never been so frightened in my life. "I've done nothing wrong."

Terri sat back in her chair, then said, "I'm sorry, but I need you to give me your name badge and pharm authorization card."

I felt like I was being stripped of my identity. I took the lanyard from around my neck and handed it to her. "This is my life."

"I know," she said softly. "As I said, there will be a formal investigation. In the meantime, you're suspended without pay. We'll see what the investigation turns up."

I just sat there, numb.

"You can go, Richelle. I'll be in touch."

I looked up at her. "I've given everything to this job."

Terri hesitated a moment, then said, "That's what I warned you about, Richelle. Any time you put all your eggs in one basket, you're just one stumble away from catastrophe."

I walked out of the unit past the other nurses without looking at them. I wondered if they already knew.

I crossed the parking lot, oblivious to everything around me. The snow hadn't slowed at all, and my car was buried beneath a thin sheet of white. I got in without brushing it off and called Justin. He answered on the first ring.

"So you miss me already?"

I started to cry.

"Richelle?"

"Something bad has happened."

"Were you in an accident? Where are you?"

"I'm at the hospital."

"What happened, Richelle?"

"I've been accused of stealing drugs."

"Who accused you?"

"The hospital. They say there are witnesses. I've been put on suspension and they took my badge. There's going to be an investigation."

"Are you okay to drive or should I come get you?"

"You have a flight."

"I'll cancel it. Do I need to come get you?"

"I can drive."

"Be careful. I'll be waiting."

---

The drive home was a blur. I remember waiting at a traffic light wiping my eyes, then looking over at a man in the car next to me who was staring at me. Then, bizarrely, he put his fingers on the outside corners of his eyes and pulled them back. I assume he was trying to make fun of my being Chinese.

As I pulled into the driveway, Justin walked out to meet me. I fell into his arms. After a few minutes he said, "Come on inside. It's cold." He walked me inside the house and led me to the couch. "I'll make you some hot tea."

"Don't leave me," I said.

"I won't," he said, sitting down with me. He looked at me seriously. "Tell me exactly what happened."

"As soon as I got to work I went in to see Terri to ask her for Christmas off. She said she was waiting for me to get in to talk to me. She told me that several sources had said they'd witnessed me stealing drugs."

"Did she tell you who accused you?"

"No. She said she couldn't. But they've started an investigation."

He pulled me close to him as I broke down crying again. After I'd calmed some I said, "I'm scared."

"I know," he said softly. "But it will be okay."

"I could lose everything. My job, my license. I could go to jail."

"That's not going to happen. You didn't do anything wrong. They can't punish you for something you didn't do."

"Innocent people go to jail."

"You're not going to jail. I promise."

"I don't understand why someone would accuse me of stealing drugs."

"Probably because *they* were the ones stealing drugs, and they were about to be caught." He thought a moment, then said, "I'll call my brother and see what he has to say about this. He'll know what to do."

I laid my head back against his chest. He put his arms around me. The stress and fear were more than my consciousness could handle. I closed my eyes and fell asleep.

# CHAPTER

## *twenty-four*

*There are few places more reassuring or safe than the arms of a loved one or the pages of a good book.*

*—Richelle Bach's diary*

I woke in Justin's arms. I didn't know how long I'd been out, but I'd slept deep enough that I didn't know where I was or what time it was. Then the weight of the accusation returned, as heavy on my chest as a sack of concrete.

"You didn't leave me," I said softly.

"I'll never leave you."

"Even if I go to jail?"

He lifted my face to look at him. "You're not going to jail."

"I'm just scared."

"I know." A moment later he said, "We need to get out of here. Let's go to the library. There are thousands of distractions there."

We drove to the Holladay Library, where we held our Calliope Writers Group meetings. Bill, the library's assistant director, saw me enter and asked if there was a Calliope event he didn't know about. I told him I was there on my own time.

I went to my favorite section of the library, the shelves with the young adult novels. I browsed through the books until I found one I thought I could get lost in, a book called *Love & Gelato*, which, from the first page, I knew I would like.

I took the book, then found Justin on the other side of the library perusing the history section. He was holding a book on World War II and *The Rise and Fall of the Third Reich*. We couldn't have been further apart on the literary spectrum.

Justin dragged two beanbag chairs together and we fell into them and lost ourselves. It was a much-needed diversion, and it was dark outside when I set my book down, having read the entire thing in one sitting.

"How was your book?" he asked.

"Really good."

"Did it have a happy ending?"

I nodded. "Yes. Did yours?"

# CHAPTER

## *twenty-five*

*When Michelle and I were small, our dad took us to an amusement park
with a kiddie car ride. The little plastic cars had spinning steering wheels
that didn't do anything except give us the illusion of control. Just like
life. As much as we like to think we're in charge and no matter how fast
or intentionally we spin our wheels, our destiny just stubbornly grinds
along its own concrete track.*

—*Richelle Bach's diary*

Neither of us wanted to cook, so I told Justin about an obscure little hole-in-the-wall Chinese restaurant in a nearby strip mall, tucked between a chiropractor and a hair salon. It was called the Cheng Li Tea House. My father had told me that *cheng li* in Mandarin means "victory," which is why so many streets and schools in Taiwan are named Cheng Li.

The restaurant was dimly lit, the walls covered with Chinese *Gwo Hwa*s, paintings on silk of the Chinese countryside. Crimson red and gold lanterns hung from the ceiling next to banners with Chinese characters.

Adding to the visual cacophony were Christmas

decorations—a Christmas tree hung with Chinese takeout boxes for baubles and a dragon with a Santa hat. Against one wall there was a small Santa doll nailed to a cross. I think we both noticed it at the same time.

"That's disturbing," Justin said.

"I'm surprised no one has ever told them it's weird."

"Maybe it's new."

"It looks old," I said. "I don't think they understand the Christmas connection between Santa and Jesus."

"I'm not sure that I do either," he said.

We followed a small, slightly stooped, elderly Asian woman to a table. She turned to me and said, *"Ni yau bu yau dzwo dzai jeli?"*

"I'm sorry. I don't speak Chinese."

She looked at me scornfully, as if I'd betrayed my ethnicity by not speaking the mother tongue. "Do you want to sit here?" she asked in heavily accented English.

*"Je li ben hau,"* Justin said.

*"Hau,"* the woman answered. She set our menus down on the table, then scurried off.

After we'd sat down, I said, "I thought you said *wo ai ni* was the extent of your Chinese."

"I said that was *about* the extent of my Chinese. I know a few more words."

"Like what?"

"I can't say."

"Why?"

"I think they might get us kicked out of here."

I smiled.

The woman brought us water in cups made from bamboo.

"Do you get that often?" Justin asked. "People talking to you in Chinese?"

"No. But it's the second time it's happened here. Just after my father got sick, he brought me here for dinner. Apparently, he came here a lot with my mother when Michelle and I were babies. He said they had great pot stickers and hot and sour soup.

"When we walked in the hostess started speaking to me in Mandarin. I didn't understand what she was saying, but my father did, which really messed with her mind."

"How well did your father speak Mandarin?"

"He was comfortable with it. He studied Chinese while he lived in Taiwan. By the time he left the island, he spoke almost fluently."

In homage to my father, we ordered a plate of pot stickers and two bowls of hot and sour soup, then a dish of chicken fried rice and kung pao shrimp.

While we were eating our soup, I told Justin, "My father told me when he lived in Taiwan he had hot and sour soup almost every day. He claimed it could cure colds.

"When he got back to America it didn't taste the same. One day he mentioned this to my mother. She said, 'That's because it's not the same in America. It doesn't have *zhu xue*.' He said, 'What's *zhu xue*?' She said, 'Pig's blood.' The little black things he thought were mushrooms were actually curdled drops of pig's blood."

Justin looked down at the black drops in his soup. "I think I'll pass on this." He pushed the bowl to the side. As we waited for our meals, Justin asked, "Do you ever wonder what all these Chinese characters mean?"

"Not really. I just think of them as art."

"Chinese calligraphy is a form of art," he said. "But there's also a lot of ancient wisdom contained in those characters."

"You sound like my father," I said. "Along with the language he studied Buddhism, Taoism, and Chinese philosophy. He once shared a Chinese proverb I never forgot: *An invisible thread connects those who are destined to meet, regardless of time, place, and circumstance. The thread may stretch or tangle, but it will never break.*"

"I like that."

"Maybe that's us."

"Maybe," he said. "Maybe."

We ordered a dessert of egg tarts and chocolate-dipped fortune cookies. As we were finishing up I said to him, "Thank you."

"For what?"

"Watching over me. Distracting me."

"It's my pleasure. How are you feeling?"

"A little better. I'm still worried."

"I'm worried too. Not because I don't think things will work out. I'm just worried about you having to go through all this."

"You really think things will work out?"

"I'm certain of it."

"I wish I could believe that. It just feels like every time things start going well for me, something bad happens. My life doesn't look at all like I thought it would."

Justin laced his fingers together. "That's the great secret of the universe," he said. "No one's life does. Not yours, certainly not mine."

"Sometimes I just wonder where I would have been if James and I had just gotten married."

Justin's brow furrowed. "Well, we wouldn't be here right now. So there's that."

I smiled a little. "That's true."

"I know, small consolation, right?"

"No. It's not small," I said.

We were both silent for a moment, then he said, "I think that had you married James, you'd still be right here."

"What do you mean?"

"James was an accident waiting to happen."

I suddenly felt defensive. "You've never even met James."

"No, but his actions speak for themselves, don't they? What kind of man sleeps with his fiancée's sister, knowing he would destroy two relationships? You'd have to be pretty self-absorbed to even think about that. Or worse, to *not* think about that." He looked at me. "Am I wrong?"

I didn't like the questions or where they led. "James had a healthy *self-interest*."

Justin shook his head. "That's what I thought. Maybe your sister did you a favor."

"Don't say that," I said. "What she did was awful. Why are we even talking about this?"

"I don't think you've ever considered that things might not be the way you see them."

I felt myself growing more defensive. "What *way* is that?"

"I'll give you an example. I had a cousin who married this guy from Louisiana. Textbook narcissist. It didn't take long for him to show his true colors.

"The longer they were together, the more abusive he became. Since I only saw her occasionally, witnessing her decline was like watching a time lapse video. She looked different every time I saw her. She kept getting thinner and frailer. He made her have plastic surgery to fix all the flaws he saw in her. He was literally draining the life out of her.

"It was obvious to everyone that something was wrong. But if anyone tried to talk to her about him, she would get defensive and turn on them. She said she was only being loyal, defending her man like any good wife would. But she wasn't defending her man—the creep was indefensible—she was defending her ego. To admit that she'd made that big a mistake was more painful than enduring the abuse.

"It took her almost a decade before she got out. After all those years of suffering I barely recognized her. She was a broken, bitter woman. Whenever we talked, it was about how much she hated the guy. Even divorced he still had a hold over her.

"It took a while for her to understand that as angry as she was at him, deep inside, she was just as angry at herself for wasting all those precious years defending and caring for a man who only cared about himself. It was only after she admitted that to herself that she began to heal. And to trust again."

"You don't think I have the right to be angry at my sister?"

"It has nothing to do with rights. It doesn't even have anything to do with your sister. She's gone. You're not. What you hold on to is all about you. We all create personal narratives. Whether they're true or not doesn't even matter, because in matters of the heart, believing makes it so. I just don't want you to believe a narrative that brings you pain the rest of your life."

"What narrative is that?"

"That your sister hated you."

"She did."

"You don't know that."

"I know that in six years she never apologized to me. I think that's a pretty good sign."

"Maybe she didn't believe she deserved your forgiveness."

"You didn't know my sister."

His eyes took on an instant intensity. "Maybe she just never felt she was as good as you."

"You really don't know my sister," I said, shaking my head. "She always thought she was better than me. She always had more friends than me. More boyfriends than me. She was fun, I was boring."

"She thought that or you did?"

"Everyone did."

"You know, Richelle, you'd be a tough act for anyone to follow. But for a twin, to be constantly compared to you, that would be a nightmare."

I wasn't sure how to respond. It's hard defending yourself against a compliment. "I don't understand why you're defending her."

"I'm not. I'm defending you."

"From whom?"

"From yourself."

I exhaled. "Well, she'd be happy now, watching me crash and burn."

"You're not going to crash and burn, Richelle. We're going to beat this thing. Together. I promise. I won't leave you."

I breathed out heavily. "I'm sorry I got so defensive."

"No, it's my fault. I wasn't trying to back you into a corner. I'm just a fixer. I want you to be happy."

"I know."

"Are you ready to go?"

"Yes."

Justin paid for our meal, then drove us back to my house. As we walked in he asked, "Can you sleep?"

"I think so. I'll take a melatonin."

He took my hand. "I hope I didn't say anything too painful tonight."

"You gave me some things to think about. At least other than going to jail."

He shook his head. "You're not going to jail."

"I believe you." I kissed him. "Thank you for everything today. I can't imagine what it would be like to go through this alone."

"You won't have to."

═══════

Looking back, I wish he'd been right.

# CHAPTER

*twenty-six*

*Justin and I went to Sugarhouse Park today to go tubing. It's the same park that my father would take Michelle and me to when we were little. He would usually bring a book to read while we would swing or climb on the monkey bars. I'll never forget when a woman, thinking we were alone and likely worried about the lone man sitting next to the playground, asked where our mother was. Michelle looked at her and said, "Who cares?" The woman walked away without a word.*

—*Richelle Bach's diary*

## SATURDAY, DECEMBER 14

The next morning, I woke late. Again. It was becoming a habit. Or, maybe, a coping mechanism. Any time spent sleeping was time I wasn't in emotional pain. Still, I felt like I'd been run over by a truck. "Justin?"

A moment later Justin walked into my bedroom carrying a coffee cup. He set the coffee on my nightstand. "How'd you sleep?"

"Like the dead."

"Good. You needed it." He kissed me. "How do you feel this morning?"

I shrugged.

"I know what we should do today. Something totally random."

"What do you have in mind?"

"I don't know what you call it, but the other day I drove by a park and people were sliding down hills on inner tubes. It looked fun."

"You're right, that is totally random. It's called tubing. And I don't have any tubes."

"There's a tire store on Highland Drive. I'm sure they'll have some."

I looked at him curiously. "You've really never done this."

"Where would I have? I didn't grow up around snow."

"Okay. But you don't have the right clothes. Do you have gloves or a hat?"

"No."

"Boots?"

"No."

"I have my father's things," I said. "But I doubt his boots will fit. You have pretty big feet." I looked down at his New Balance running shoes. "You're going to be cold."

"I've been cold since I got here."

"Don't say I didn't warn you."

I bundled Justin up the best I could, then we picked up an old truck inner tube from the tire store, and drove to the park. It was Saturday so the hill was crowded. Except for a few parents with small children, I think we were the oldest ones there. Justin carried our tube as we trudged to the top of the hill. We were both out of breath when we reached the small summit.

"I feel like I should plant a flag or something," he said.

I laughed. "Don't feel too cool. There are five-year-olds climbing this."

"Let's do this," he said. He sat down on one side of the tube and I sat on the other, our legs interlocked in the middle.

"How do you steer this thing?"

"You don't," I said. "You just go."

"What if someone's in the way?"

"They move. Or they get hit."

"I can see the appeal," he said.

We scooted our way forward until the tube began to move on its own. We were soon flying recklessly down the hill and not hitting a single person. When we came to a stop Justin just laid back on the tube, his whole body covered with frost. "That was fun. I can't believe I grew up without this."

"At least all this snow is good for something. Ready to go again?"

"You do it more than once?"

I laughed. "Of course. We used to tube all day."

It took only three more runs until we decided that the hike wasn't worth the ten seconds of thrill. We donated our tube to a group of teenagers, then stopped at the Dunkin' Donuts across from the park for crullers and hot chocolate, then drove home.

After we had shed our winter shells, I took a hot bath while Justin showered downstairs, then took a short nap. When he finally got up, I was making turkey sandwiches from the meat left over from our Thanksgiving. I cut the sandwiches and we sat down to eat.

"Olivia would love tubing," Justin said. "She loves thrills. Like her mother."

I smiled. "How is Olivia?"

"She's good. I talked to her this morning before you got up."

"Texas is an hour ahead?"

"Yes. She was watching cartoons."

"How long did you tell her you were staying?"

"I didn't."

"How long are you staying?"

"For as long as you need me."

I felt a rush of gratitude. "Thank you. But I'll be okay. You can't just leave Olivia. She needs you too."

"She'll be all right. She has my mother and father. I'm pretty sure she likes her farmor and farfar more than me."

"What did you call them?"

"Farmor and farfar. It's Swedish. Olivia says, 'Grandpa is *farmor* fun than my father.'"

"I doubt that."

"It's true. Grandparents have a definite advantage over parents. It's the old good-cop-bad-cop routine. Grandparents always get to be the good cop. I'm the one who has to tell her no."

"You sound like a really good father. You should go home to her. I'll be okay."

"We can talk about it tomorrow," he said.

"All right. Tomorrow."

"We've tubed," he said. "Got that off my bucket list. What should we do now?"

"We could play cards," I said. "Or a board game. I have a lot of those."

We walked over to a cupboard filled with my father's old games. A few of them were vintage, like Twister and Mouse Trap.

"We could play Monopoly," I said.

"No," Justin said. "Monopoly's no fun with two people. You just end up hating each other. How about Scrabble?"

"You sure you want to play Scrabble against an author?"

"Are you sure you want to play against a rocket scientist?"

"Oh, it's on," I said. "Prepare to learn the alphabet."

"Trash talk from the nurse," he said. "This is going to be fun."

We set the game up on the dining room table.

"I'll go first," I said. "You can eat my tiles."

"More trash talk. Where did all this aggression come from?"

"It's been bottled up for years," I said. "I get very competitive at games."

We had been playing for about twenty minutes when Justin laid down five tiles.

M-I-C-K-I.

"That's thirteen points," he said. "The K is worth five."

"You can't use that. It's not even a word."

"Of course it is. Ever heard of Mickey Mouse?"

"Yes, and it's a name. You can't use names. Haven't you ever played this before?"

"Where does it say you can't use names?"

I grabbed the rules. "Right here. Words that are spelled with a capital letter cannot be used. That means names."

"What if I don't spell it with a capital letter?"

"It doesn't matter."

"You used PAT."

"Pat's a verb. As in pat a dog on the head. Or a noun: a pat of butter."

"*And* Pat Sajak. It's also a name."

"If it's a verb, you can use it."

"Show me where it says that."

"It doesn't have a capital. Besides, you don't spell Mickey like that anyway."

"Michelle did."

Everything in my head stopped. The two simple words hung in the air between us.

He looked as surprised by what he said as I was.

"How did you know that?" As I looked at him I suddenly understood. "You knew her."

He said nothing.

"Did you know Michelle?"

He breathed out slowly. "Yes."

My mind flooded with a thousand questions. It took a moment to select one. "Were you one of her boyfriends?"

He hesitated for a long time, then said, "I was her husband."

I sat there, my mind reeling through this new labyrinth. "Michelle is the wife you lost?"

He nodded.

". . . And Olivia?"

"She's your niece."

I felt like I'd just been let in on some horrible prank. I didn't even know that Michelle was married, let alone had a baby. "You said you were divorced."

"No. You just thought that."

"But you never corrected me."

"There was no point."

"No point?" I stepped back from the table. "All this time, you already knew everything about me. Yet you asked me . . ." I stopped, filled with indignation. "Have you been in this house before?"

"Yes."

"Oh, this just keeps getting better. Did you know my father?"

He didn't answer.

"Did you?"

"Not well, but Michelle and I visited him several times. He came out when Olivia was born."

"My father was in on this?"

He looked at me quizzically. "In on *what*?"

"He never told me he saw Michelle."

"You expected him to disown her just because you did? Michelle asked him not to. He respected her wishes."

"At my expense."

"At what expense, Richelle? How would your knowing that have made your life better?"

"A little honesty would have been nice." I exhaled. "That's how you knew about . . . where I lived. About the plane my father flew."

"What I said about the plane was true. Your father was impressed."

I just glared at him. "At least something you said was true. What are you even doing here?"

"It's complicated."

"No, it's not. What were you doing, trying to replace my sister with a look-alike? Take another goldfish home to fool your child?"

"That's not fair. It's not like that."

"What is it like?" I asked angrily. "Why did you come here?"

"I came to fulfill a promise to Michelle."

"What promise?" I crossed my arms, waiting for the explanation.

"A Christmas promise," he said. "Last year I asked Michelle what she wanted for Christmas. She said, 'I want my sister back.' Then out of nowhere she asked me to make her a promise that if something ever happened to her, that I would give you her opal." He reached into his pocket and brought out a small black velvet jewelry box. He opened it to reveal the black opal pendant my father had given to Michelle on the night of our graduation. I thought she had sold it when she was stuck in Europe.

"She wanted you to have it to remember her by."

I didn't take the pendant from him. After a moment he closed the box and put it back in his pocket.

"I should have brought it sooner. But I was grieving. I'd just lost my wife. And Olivia needed me. But when I was able to start breathing again, I wanted to fulfill her wish.

"I didn't tell you because I knew how angry you were at her. My plan was to just come to Utah and leave the next day. But whenever I came by the house, you weren't home. I came by six times that day. Then I extended my stay an extra day, but you still didn't answer the door. You probably were home but thought I was a solicitor. That's when I remembered that Michelle had told me about your writing group."

"How did she know about that?"

"She followed you on social media."

"She stalked me?"

Justin looked angry. "It was more like trying to hold on to you. It was the only way she could have you in her life."

I didn't know what to say.

"So, I went to your writers club. My plan was to wait until the meeting was over, then introduce myself, hand you the opal, and go home. But when I saw you . . ." Justin looked down for a moment before speaking. "You can't imagine how that affected me. Try to put yourself in my place, Richelle. If you had lost the person you loved the most in your life, then suddenly you saw them again."

"You didn't see her. You saw me."

"Yes. And after all Michelle had said about you, I felt like I knew you. And I wanted to get to know you even better."

"What did she say about me? I was rigid?"

He slowly shook his head. "She said you were the woman she always wanted to be."

I let his words fade into silence.

"It was you who didn't know your sister, Richelle. She loved you."

"You're going to start defending her again?"

"Someone should. Michelle paid for what she did. A thousand times over. It's time you knew the truth."

"The truth," I snapped. "You're going to start telling the truth now?"

He took a deep breath. Even with the intensity of my emotion, his voice was calm. "As long as I knew her, Michelle never once said anything bad about you. Not once. In fact, she idolized you. She idolized your strength and discipline. She idolized your goodness. She said you were the good one and she was the screwup. She even had a tattoo on her wrist that said 'the wrong one.' Did you ever wonder about that?"

The truth was, I hadn't even noticed it.

"She felt that way her whole life. She pretended that being the lesser twin didn't bother her, but it did. Deeply. She told me exactly what you said, that she wouldn't have even graduated from high school if it wasn't for you. She spent her whole life trying to keep up with you until she finally accepted that she couldn't. That's why she left for Europe. She couldn't stand the constant comparison anymore. She was tired of being the 'evil' twin everyone joked about. It hurt her every time." His brow fell. "Did you ever tell her you were proud of her?"

The words stung. Michelle had complimented me more times than I could possibly remember. I couldn't think of a single time I'd given her even a little praise. I responded defensively. "So that's why she slept with my fiancée. She just admired me so much?"

He breathed out slowly. "Yes, there was that." He looked out with dark eyes. "You know, she really did do you a favor."

"She did me a favor by derailing my marriage?"

He nodded slightly. "Michelle didn't go to James. He went to her."

"That's why I found her in his bed?"

"It was all his idea, Richelle. You may not want to believe that, but it was."

"And you know this how?"

"I know every horrid detail of that night. I got so sick of Michelle confessing what an awful person she was that I asked if there was a statute of limitations on mistakes or if it was a life sentence. She said she couldn't let it go until you did."

I just looked at him.

"That night, she was alone in her room, heavily medicated for her migraine. You're a nurse—you know migraine medications can muddle your thinking."

I did know.

"That's when James knocked on her door. He asked her if she could come to his room to see a gift he had gotten you for Christmas. She said she didn't feel well and asked if it could wait, but he said it was urgent that she see it before you came back.

"When they got to his room he went after her. She told him to keep away, but he kept after her. He told her that she was the fun one—the one he really wanted to be with.

"She wasn't thinking right, Richelle. But even then, for once she had someone choose her over you. It was in that moment of weakness that she fell. She listened to him, to prove to herself that she could have something you had. Even for a minute."

Justin breathed out heavily. "I'm not saying it's right, but if you think you hated her for what she'd done, it was nothing compared to the hate she piled on herself. She regretted what she'd done every day of her life."

"So moving in together was also an accident?"

"They didn't go to California together. Michelle exiled herself. She moved to California to run away from her mistake. And your peerless James chased her. She was lonely and broken and had no one else, so she let him stay for a while, but it barely lasted a week. She broke off the relationship, not him. She hated him for talking her into hurting you.

"After she threw him out, her life went into a spiral. That's when I met her. I was meeting a few of my colleagues for an after-work drink when I noticed her sitting alone at the bar, drinking. She had clearly had too much to drink, and there was some creep trying to take advantage of her. He kept touching her and she tried to push him away. That's when I intervened.

"I ended up driving her home and putting her to bed. I called her the next day to check on her and we had a long talk. She wanted to thank me, so we went to dinner. That started our relationship. After several weeks, she told me what she'd done to you and confided in me that she had planned to take her life that night I met her. She even showed me the suicide note she'd written asking for your forgiveness.

"I told her that she needed to reach out to you. I pleaded with her, but she wouldn't. She said she had no right to ask your forgiveness or even be in your life anymore. She believed that when you were ready, you would reach out to her." He took a slow, deep breath. "But you never did."

"So now it's my fault?"

His voice softened. "I'm not looking for blame, Richelle. You can decide that. I'm just telling you what happened."

"What about my father? She didn't even come to his funeral."

"I know. She stayed in bed and wept. I had to force her to eat. She loved your father, Richelle. As much as you did. And he loved her. I begged her to go to the funeral. Do you know what she said? She said, 'I can't do that to Richelle. She was closer to him than I was. She was his favorite. I can't ruin it for her.' "

Again, I didn't know what to say to that. "So, this whole time, you hid all this from me?"

"I told you there were things I wasn't ready to share with you."

"That was a pretty big *thing*. How did you think I was going to react to this?"

"I had no idea. After I found myself falling for you, I kept putting it off. I was afraid it might drive you away, and I wanted to be with you."

"Why? So you could *pretend* you hadn't lost her? You used me. You two were perfect for each other."

His expression turned angry. "Tell me, Richelle. How did I use you?"

I couldn't answer him. Finally, I said, "I want you to go." The words rang out like a bell, their ugliness ringing into silence. I could see the sadness in his eyes.

"You want me to leave?"

"Yes."

He quietly looked at me for a moment, then suddenly exhaled deeply. "Are you sure that's what you want?"

I swallowed. Even though it wasn't, I said, "Yes."

Justin just looked at me for a moment, then said, "All right." He walked over and set the black velvet jewelry box down on the counter, then walked out into the living room and picked his coat up from the arm of the sofa. He turned to me. "I wasn't pretending anything, Richelle. I really do love you. I'm sorry you don't believe that." He turned back toward the door.

His love hurt more than his anger. In my pain I shouted, "I never want to see you again."

He stopped at the door and turned back. "Same last words you said to your sister. Maybe you should be more careful about what you wish for."

He opened the door and walked out into the cold. The sound of the door shutting behind him was like the closing of a tomb. I thought I was lonely before. I had no idea how deep that hole could go.

I fell to my knees sobbing. "Daddy."

# CHAPTER

## *twenty-seven*

*God hates me.*

*—Richelle Bach's diary*

## DECEMBER 15–21

The next week passed in a frigid, barren, and icy haze. I had never felt so cold in all my life. It wasn't all the weather, but still it seemed as if the climate had conspired with life to make me suffer. A freezing arctic front had come from thousands of miles away down into the Salt Lake Valley, freezing everything in its path.

With no work, I just wallowed in the nightmare that had become my life. In my anger I tried working on the *Prodigal Daughter* book, but nothing came. Maybe it was just the hypocrisy of it all. If even part of what Justin had said was true, I was just piling more shame on someone who wanted nothing more than to be loved by me. Yeah, I felt pretty awful.

I realized just how much I had relied on work to distract me from my chronic loneliness and existential crisis. I had always chosen the sickest patients to care for. I told myself I did this because I was a good and caring person. Now, I felt neither good nor caring. Maybe I never had been. Maybe the only reason I did it was because seeing others in real life-and-death struggles helped dilute the intensity of my own pain.

Something else nagged at me. Why hadn't anyone from work called? Were all my relationships really that shallow? Didn't anyone care about me?

As much as I feared the investigation, in so many ways losing Justin felt equally painful. Maybe even more so. At least with the hospital I could claim innocence. But not with him. In the heat of the moment, it had been easy to discount what he said—but now, in the solitude of my thoughts, his words began to sink in. *What if everything he said was true?* Was it really too hard to believe that James had initiated the affair? Or had I, deep inside, known all along, but didn't want to accept that he didn't love me and probably never had? James was arrogant and self-centered, something I shrouded with the label of self-confidence. Cheating on me wasn't below him. And I had never felt as loved by James as I had by Justin. Not even close. In my confused emotional state, I wanted Justin to hold me, even comfort me for the mess I had created in hurting him.

The holiday moved around me like a party I hadn't been invited to, like a song playing in someone else's car. The Christmas tree that Justin and I had decorated felt like sacrilege. I unplugged its lights so I noticed it less, but even that didn't help much. I probably would have taken it down, but I didn't have the energy.

The pain of the unknown was slowly breaking me, the hospital investigation's outcome hanging perilously over me like the heavy blade of a guillotine, ready to fall at any moment. For better or worse, part of me just wanted the whole thing over with.

I made the mistake of looking up my alleged crime and actual punishment on the internet. In the battle against the opioid epidemic, lawmakers had created severe punishments for those involved in the trade. Selling opioids was a felony. In addition to losing my job and nursing license, which was painfully staggering in itself, if convicted, I could face up to four years in jail and a $20,000 fine. The thought of that triggered seismic panic attacks. That wasn't possible, was it? The question that nagged me most was *who were the witnesses?*

With the exception of a few unwelcomed telemarketers, my phone remained conspicuously silent. I anticipated that any day I would be receiving a phone call from the hospital with the verdict. Or would police just show up at my door and haul me away? What would happen to my house? Aside from an accidental speeding ticket, which the officer mercifully changed to a warning, I had never been in trouble with the law. I had no idea how the process worked.

Wednesday the eighteenth, a week before Christmas, my phone rang. The call was from the hospital. My heart raced. *Was the jury back? Was this really it?* I wished my father was there to protect me. He was a warrior. He would stand in the way of the storm. I had never felt so alone in all my life.

"Hello?"

"Richelle, this is Amelia. I just heard what happened. Are you okay?"

I breathed out in relief. "No. I'm not. I can't believe this is happening to me."

"Neither can I," she said. "You're the best nurse I know. Terri's pretty hush-hush about everything. Do you know what's going on?"

"She said they're doing some kind of investigation."

"How long will that take?"

"I don't know. I really don't know anything."

"I'm so sorry," she said. "How long until they let you back?"

"Maybe never," I said.

"Never?" she repeated. "Is your boyfriend with you?"

The question hurt. "No. He left me."

"Because of this?"

"No. I sent him away."

"I'm so sorry," she said again. "When it rains it pours. Keep hopeful, Richelle. Everything will be all right. I'm praying for you, honey."

"Thank you, Amelia. You don't know how much it means to me that you called. You're the only one at the hospital who's reached out to me. I feel like a pariah."

"You're not a pariah. In huddle they warned us not to talk to you. It's hospital policy."

"They told you not to talk to me?"

"It's policy."

"You broke policy to call me?"

"We're friends, honey. You've always been there for me. Besides, what are they going to do, fire me?"

"They could."

"You can't fire slaves," she said. "Besides, that's what friends are for. And for the record, no one here thinks you did anything wrong."

"It was someone there who accused me."

Amelia went silent. "Someone in our unit? Who would do that?"

"Terri won't tell me."

"If I find out who it is, I'll let you know. After I take off their head. I'm so sorry. But you hang in there. Everything will work out."

"I wish I could believe that."

"Have faith, Richelle. You're a good person."

"Thank you for reaching out, Amelia. I love you."

"I love you too. Hang in there. We're all pulling for you. And if you need anything, just call. Take care, now. Bye."

"Bye." I slowly hung up. At least someone cared.

# CHAPTER

*twenty-eight*

*The people in our lives are like cards in a deck. At different times we draw, hold, and discard, but, in the end, we don't really know the cards' value until life calls our hand.*

—*Richelle Bach's diary*

## SUNDAY, DECEMBER 22

Sunday morning I braved the cold and the world and went to church alone. The church was beautifully lit with candles, and the parishioners were dressed a little nicer than usual.

The pastor had prepared a special Christmas sermon, punctuated with beautiful Christmas music. Christmas hymns have always brought me comfort, and even in the storm of the moment, my heart felt some peace.

After the service had started, a thin young woman with jet-black hair sat down next to me. She was a little different looking. Edgy. She wore tall black leather boots and had a half dozen piercings in her right ear. When she took off her coat she only had on a light, low-cut blouse, exposing her tattooed arms.

I suppose it wasn't too peculiar that she sat next to me, since the auditorium was almost completely full. There were always more people at church during Christmas. My father jokingly called them the C&E crowd—Christmas and Easter Christians. He never said that in a judgmental way. In fact, I think he was more amused by the phenomenon than anything. It was just human nature. He told me a joke once about a church that was infested with mice. The pastor and his staff tried traps and exterminators, all to no avail. Finally, the pastor grabbed a hose and said, "Let's baptize them. At least that way they'll only show up on Christmas and Easter." My father liked that joke. I guess I was now part of that crowd.

During the sermon the tattooed woman abruptly turned to me and asked if I was okay. I lied. I wasn't about to share what I was going through with a total stranger. Then, to my surprise, she said, "Be still, sister. God is God." That's all she said.

———

The young woman's words were still on my mind that afternoon when my phone rang. I was horizontal on the couch reading and set aside my book to see who was calling. It was the hospital. The fear returned in full force. I suppose this was how a defendant felt waiting for the jury's verdict. Everything in my life could change in the next minute.

Mustering my courage, I took a deep breath and picked up the phone. "Hello."

"Richelle, it's Terri."

I swallowed. "Is the investigation over?"

"Yes. I just heard from the administration. You've been cleared of all wrongdoing."

I let the impact of her words settle. "Just like that?"

"Just like that. And I need to formally state that, on behalf of MRH, I apologize for any inconvenience this might have caused you."

"Inconvenience? Waiting on the phone for a doctor is an inconvenience. This could have destroyed my life."

"I'm sorry, Richelle. That's what I had to say for our records. As your friend, I can't tell you how sorry I am. I can't imagine the pain this has caused you. I never believed you had done anything wrong."

"You could have fooled me."

"I know, and it hurts my heart. I had to play it that way. Professionally, I couldn't show bias, but behind the scenes, I advocated for you wherever I could."

"I understand," I said. "Thank you for making this go away."

"I'd like to take credit, but I can't. To tell you the truth, in all my years at the hospital, I've never seen anything like this. Unless you have some high-level political connections I don't know about, you have angels watching over you."

"Why do you say that?"

"The Utah DEA contacted our administration to say they were taking over the investigation. They actually sent an undercover agent inside the hospital to investigate."

"Is that unusual?"

"Unusual doesn't begin to describe it. The DEA has never meddled with our affairs. We still don't know how they even found out about it."

*Justin*, I thought. *He called his brother.*

"They basically ran a sting operation. These guys know what they're doing. The first day the agent bought opioids from one of the guilty parties. From what I've been told, he was so terrified at being caught that he confessed to everything and informed on his accomplice."

"There was more than one person involved?"

"There were two."

"How did the DEA know who to approach?"

"They started by investigating the witnesses. And their hunch was right. Apparently, one of the pharm techs had noticed some irregularities and filed a report. Your accusers got scared and looked for someone to push the blame on. I guess you were the most convenient."

"Who were they?"

Terri hesitated for a moment, then said, "Technically I'm not supposed to tell you, but after what they put you through, I don't care about protecting them. It was your colleague Amelia and a pharm tech on the fifth floor named Guy Snell."

I couldn't believe it. "Amelia," I said. ". . . and Guy."

"I know you know Amelia, but do you know the guy?"

"He used to come down to see me every day."

"According to the DEA's report, Amelia was the instigator. She's an opioid addict."

*That's why she kept calling in sick*, I thought.

"Apparently, she was dating this Guy character and duped the poor schmuck into doing her bidding."

In spite of all Guy had put me through, I actually felt sorry for him.

"Amelia was the last one I would have suspected," I said. "She called just a few days ago to console me. She told me she loved me."

"It's like they say, never trust an addict. They lie to everyone. Beginning with themselves."

I breathed out slowly. "So now what?"

"Well, you've been through a lot. Frankly, I wouldn't blame you for leaving the hospital after all that, but I hope you'll stay with us. You're one of the finest nurses I've ever worked with."

"I wasn't planning on leaving."

"You don't know how glad I am to hear that. So, as far as your schedule, according to hospital policy, you'll be given back pay for time lost. Then I got the higher-ups to throw in the rest of the year off with pay. If that's okay, you'll start back up again in January. I'll call you after I complete next month's schedule."

"Thank you," I said.

"Well, again, I'm not the one to thank. Someone up there loves you."

*And someone in Texas.*

# CHAPTER

*twenty-nine*

*There are times when the unseen hand of the universe pulls a lever*
*and a fifty-pound switch changes the course of a ten-thousand-ton*
*locomotive. So it is in life. In my case, I know who threw the switch.*
*I just don't know why.*

*—Richelle Bach's diary*

In my college years, the day after finals I would usually come down with a cold or the flu. It was as if my body had pulled every bit of energy to meet the crisis, and then, once it was over, deflated. After the call I collapsed in bed.

A whole school of thoughts swam through my head. I wanted to call Justin to thank him, but after how badly I'd treated him, I knew I couldn't do that. The biggest question on my mind was why he would still go to such great lengths to help me. The only answer I could come up with was that he meant it when he said he loved me.

But why hadn't he just told me everything to begin with? Why couldn't he just have been honest with me? That's when I realized that the one man whose love I had never questioned, my father, hadn't told me everything either—about Michelle's marriage or her having a child or even their visits to him. There was no reason for him to hide any of that, at least not any that could have benefited him.

As I considered his motives, I realized the truth. My father wasn't protecting himself. He was protecting me from *myself*— from the most self-loathing, envious, and destructive parts of my personality. He knew that in denying Michelle my love I was denying myself hers. Deep inside I must have known it too. It was right there in my dream. It seemed so obvious. How could I have been so blind?

Once I looked past my fears, I could see Justin for who he really was—a good man like my father. A man worth fighting for. He had taken that risk with me; I could do the same.

*What if he spurned me?* Being rejected by him was far more likely than being received with open arms. But what he had once said to me was true—the greatest hurt isn't to lose love, it's the regret of never having it. It would be far better to be turned away at the door—to face his rejection—than to spend the rest of my life wondering what might have happened if I hadn't tried.

Even if he didn't want me, at least he would know that I did love him and I would be forever grateful for all he'd done for me.

I got up out of bed and walked into Michelle's room. It felt different. I knew it wasn't the room, it was my heart. As I looked around, I was filled with the strongest sense of loss I had felt since I learned of her death. For the first time I allowed myself to grieve my twin.

"I'm sorry, Micki." Tears filled my eyes as I walked over to her dresser and lifted the picture I'd turned onto its face.

There was my sister, her hands outstretched, her face filled with excitement and joy in the fall into the unknown.

How had I not seen that she was brilliant in a different way? My father did. That's why he said what he did when he gave us the opals. He didn't mean it for her, he meant it for me. Michelle embraced her fire. She knew how to drink from the wine of life, to laugh and cry and love. She knew how to live. Maybe I wasn't as smart as I thought I was.

As I stood there a wild thought came to me, something that, to this day, I can only wonder at. Was it possible that Michelle asked Justin to make that promise not to give me the gem but to give me *him*, the most precious thing she had found in her life? What if she thought it was her last chance at restitution?

I picked up my phone and called the airline.

# CHAPTER

## *thirty*

*It's a humbling moment to look in the mirror only to see a fool gazing back. I'm going to see Justin with the expectation of offering him the gratitude he's earned and receiving the punishment I deserve. Reasonably, I can't hope he'll take me back. But I can hope for grace. And true grace is rarely reasonable.*

*—Richelle Bach's diary*

The travel gods must have been smiling on me. In my sudden desire to see Justin, I hadn't considered that, regardless of my intentions, the day would still be among the busiest travel days of the year. Every flight from Salt Lake City to Dallas was booked and overbooked. Then, a kind airline employee found a last-minute open seat on a flight to Phoenix with a connection to Dallas. I booked it.

The flight to Phoenix left the next morning at 10:12 a.m. I brought only a small rolling carry-on. Frankly, I had no idea how long I would be staying. A day? A week? Thirty seconds?

It hadn't been hard to find his parents' address. There aren't a whole lot of Eks in Dallas.

The first leg of my journey was less than ninety minutes,

and I arrived at Phoenix Sky Harbor International Airport a little before noon. Even though I never left the terminal I could see that the weather was relatively balmy. I had a three-hour layover, so I got myself some lunch, then waited at the gate, watching the crowds jostle around the airport like a river of Class V rapids.

My flight to Dallas departed at 2:47 and touched down two and a half hours later at DFW. Dallas is an hour ahead of Mountain Time, so I adjusted my watch forward. It was almost 6:30 and already dark outside.

The Dallas terminal was even more crowded than Phoenix's was, and once I passed through security there were joyful reunions spontaneously erupting all around me: parents welcoming their kids home from school, wives and husbands hugging their military fatigue–clad spouses, children running to aging grandparents. It both warmed and hurt my heart. I was happy for all of them, but painfully aware that there was no one there who was excited to see me, which might also be true once I reached my final destination. *Is this really a good idea?* I pushed the question from my mind. I knew the answer. No matter the outcome, it was the right thing.

I wheeled my carry-on past the crowds at the luggage carousels out to the cab lane. Once outside I unbuttoned my sweater. The taxi line was enormous, and it took me nearly an hour just to get a cab. The whole time my mind reeled through Justin's possible reactions as I made the slow, intermittent shuffle to the curb.

When I reached the cab, the driver, an older black man with a gray, stubbly beard, came around to take my bag.

"Is this all you're carrying, young lady?" he asked.

"Yes, thank you. I'm traveling light."

While he put my bag in the trunk, I climbed into the back seat. The cab smelled like pine from one of those tree-shaped air fresheners that hung next to a large wooden cross from the rearview mirror. Christmas music played. Taped to the dash below the meter were pictures of three little children.

A moment later my driver returned to his seat.

"Where can I take you this evening, young lady?"

"Lakeshore. 975 Summer Lane."

"That's not too far from here. We'll hit a little holiday traffic, so just sit back and relax. Do you mind the music?"

"No, I like it." I looked at the taxi license mounted on the Plexiglas behind his head. "Your name is Marcus?"

"Yes, ma'am."

"I'm Richelle."

"Nice to meet you, Miss Richelle."

"Nice to meet you, Mr. Marcus."

I pointed to the photographs taped to the dashboard. "Are those pictures of your children?"

"These children here?" He laughed. "No, those would be my grandchildren. Noah, Emma, and Sophia. My daughter lives in Huntsville, so unfortunately, this is as close as I'll get to them this Christmas."

"I'm sorry," I said. "The friend I'm going to see came from Huntsville."

"Right now?"

"Yes, sir."

"Huntsville, Alabama. Rocket City USA."

After we had pulled out onto the expressway Marcus said, "It's kind of chilly out there today."

I just looked out the window. "It feels warm to me."

"You must have come from somewhere cold."

"Salt Lake City. It was snowing when I left. It's always snowing."

"We don't get much of that here. Back in the eighties, I was stationed at Fort Richardson in Anchorage. I'll tell you, we got some snow there. One week we got more than four feet. I was born in Louisiana, so I never really got used to the cold. Some people have antifreeze in their blood. I don't."

"I don't either. This has been a hard winter. I don't think I've ever been so cold."

"Well, maybe you can warm up a little while you're here. Then take a little sunshine back home with you."

"I can hope," I said.

The drive from the airport was stop-and-go as Marcus negotiated his way through the traffic he'd warned me about. I was not altogether unhappy about the delay, as the closer I got to my destination the more anxious I felt. What if he wasn't even there? *Why would he want to see me?*

Forty minutes from the time we'd left the airport, Marcus pulled his cab up to the curb in front of Justin's parents' home.

The house was located in the upscale Fort Worth suburb of Lakeshore, about eight miles from the airport. It was a well-lit, beautiful, white-brick home, one level, with a peaked shingle-covered roof and an overhanging front entryway.

Marcus turned to me. "This is the place, Miss Richelle.

975 Summer Lane. That will be thirty-six dollars and twelve cents."

For a moment I just looked out the window at the house. Then I said, "Marcus, could you please keep your meter on and wait a few minutes for me? I don't know if I'll be staying or not."

"Sure thing, young lady. I can do that. Waiting time is eighteen dollars an hour."

"That's no problem," I said. "Thank you."

"Do you need your bag?"

"I'll leave it here for now. If that's okay."

"That will be okay." As I grabbed the latch to open the door, Marcus said, "Do these folks know you're coming?"

I shook my head. "No."

"Then I'll say a prayer for a happy reunion."

"Thank you, Marcus. I appreciate that."

I let myself out of the car. A textured, acid-stained concrete walkway led to the home, surrounded on both sides by beach ball–shaped kumquat trees in terra-cotta planters. The house was beautifully landscaped and immaculately manicured, the way most retirees keep their yards.

The front door was a dark wooden frame around an etched frosted-glass panel, which was brightly illuminated from the light inside.

There were three cars in the driveway, a new Mercedes Benz, a forest-green Range Rover, and a bright red Tesla sports car. I wondered if any of the cars were Justin's, a far cry from the humble rental cars he always showed up to my house in.

As I approached the home, I could hear Christmas music

coming from inside. For a moment I stood there like a diver on the precipice of a cliff. I could feel my heart pound as I pressed the doorbell, which was followed by a light, musical chime.

Through the glass, I could see the obscured form of someone walking toward the door. There was the metallic click of a lock, then the door swung open.

In the doorway stood an attractive middle-aged woman. She had blond-and-silver-streaked-hair, high cheekbones, and beautiful brown eyes. She wore a white blouse with a plunging neckline accentuating a braided silver chain and a pink sapphire necklace.

"Hi, darling, may I . . ." She stopped abruptly, raising her hand to her chest. "Oh my Lord." I had frightened her.

"I'm Richelle," I said. "I'm Michelle's twin."

"I can see that. It just caught me . . ." She breathed out. "I was told you were identical, but I wasn't prepared. Justin didn't tell us you were coming."

"I'm sorry," I said. "Justin doesn't know I'm here. I understand why that would be a little unsettling."

"No, I apologize. Please come in."

"Thank you." I stepped into the warmth of the tiled foyer. There was a bright and peaceful spirit in the home, and the music I had heard outside resonated throughout the house.

The woman shut the door behind me. "I'm Carol, Justin's mother."

"It's a pleasure meeting you, Carol."

"Justin's in the living room watching TV with Bob. I'll give him a holler."

"Thank you."

As she walked away, I looked around the house. In the room connected to the entryway was a white frosted Christmas tree with blue lights and metallic blue baubles with a chrome star perched on top.

On the wall next to the tree was a large, elaborately framed picture of Justin's entire family. Michelle was in it, standing next to Justin. She was holding their baby. She looked happy.

I turned back just as Justin walked into the foyer. He stopped when he saw me. From the look in his eyes it was clear his mother hadn't told him it was me.

"Richelle."

I swallowed. "Hi."

He just looked at me, then said, "You may be the last person I expected to see tonight." He added, "Maybe ever."

"I know. Big surprise, right? I was unpredictable for once." He didn't say anything. I rocked nervously on the balls of my feet. "I know I should have called and asked if I could come. But after I behaved so badly, I thought you would probably just say no, so I decided to take a chance. Better to ask for forgiveness than beg for permission, right?"

He still just looked at me. "Why are you here, Richelle?"

The tone of his voice grated over my heart like the blade of a snowplow. "I found out what you did for me. With the hospital and the drug charges. I wanted to thank you."

"You could have just called."

I forced a smile even though I was dying inside. "I know, I should have. But . . ." I twisted my mouth. "Why would you still do that for me?"

"It was the right thing to do."

"Of course," I said. "Right."

He continued looking at me, flaying me with his gaze.

"Well, right or not, it was very kind of you."

Justin took a deep breath. "Richelle, I would do anything to have Michelle back. But whether she's here or not, you're still her sister. That makes you family. Family looks out for each other. Michelle would have insisted that I help."

I nodded slightly. "Would you have helped anyway?"

He hesitated for a moment, then said, "Yes. You've been through enough."

The moment stalled. Finally I said, "Wow, this is awkward. Painfully. I deserve it, of course. So, uh, before I go, I'd like to ask you one more thing."

"All right." He looked at me expectantly.

My mouth was dry. "This is hard to ask. Do you think . . ." I hesitated.

"Yes?"

"Do you think there's any way that you might give me an-other chance?" My question hung in the air like a piñata, just waiting to get smacked.

Justin just looked at me. Whether he was torturing me or trying to make up his mind, I don't know, but as I was awaiting his verdict, a tiny voice said, "Mommy?"

We both looked over to see a beautiful little Asian-featured girl standing at the side of the room. Her eyes were wide with confusion. For a moment all was frozen. Then Justin quickly dropped to his knees next to her. "Olivia, this isn't Mommy. This is Mommy's twin sister. Do you remember, I told you she had a sister who looked just like her?"

The little girl's eyes darted back and forth between us. She wore a confused expression of hope and fear.

I took a step forward, then knelt down to look directly into the little girl's face. I couldn't believe her resemblance to Michelle and me when we were little girls.

"You're Olivia?"

She nodded.

"My name is Richelle. Your mommy was my twin sister. Do you know what a twin is?"

Olivia shook her head.

"A twin is when two people are born at the same time from the same mommy and they look the same. Your mommy and I were born together. That means I'm your aunt. You can call me Aunt Richelle, or Aunt Ricki. Your mommy used to call me Ricki."

Olivia just continued staring at me. I think she wanted to believe we were lying to her, that her mother had actually returned.

I turned to Justin. "I'm so sorry. I didn't think about this. I'll leave . . ."

Justin raised his hand. "Give me a minute." He turned back to his daughter. "Honey, Richelle and Mommy were sisters, just like Nora and Jane are sisters, except they're sisters who look exactly alike. Do you understand?"

Olivia nodded.

As Justin glanced up at me, I saw something new in his eyes, something I hadn't seen since I'd arrived. He turned back to his daughter. "Richelle came because she wanted to see us. Would it be okay if she stayed a little while?"

Olivia looked at me, then nodded.

"Would you like Aunt Richelle to stay with us for Christmas?"

She nodded again.

"Good," Justin said. He turned to me. "So would I." Then he smiled. "The answer to your question is yes."

My eyes welled.

"It took courage for you to come here."

"I was terrified," I confessed. I swallowed, then said in a softer voice, "But you're worth fighting for."

He smiled. He started to move to kiss me, then stopped and glanced down at Olivia.

"It's okay," I said. "I can wait." I remembered the cab. "I have a taxi outside."

"It's been waiting this whole time?"

"In case I needed to make a quick escape," I said.

He smiled. "I'll take care of it. But first, there's some family you need to meet."

"Is your brother, Liam, here?" I asked.

"Everyone's here," he said. "Kayla surprised us and came in last night." I could see how happy this made him. "Olivia, will you take Aunt Richelle to meet your farmor and farfar?"

"Yes, Papa." Olivia took my hand. "C'mon, Aunt Richelle."

As I let her pull me from the foyer, Justin said, "Richelle."

I turned back to look at him. A beautiful smile crossed his face. "Welcome back, prodigal."

# EPILOGUE

*Spoiler alert: This story ends with me loving him forever.*
        *—Richelle Bach's diary*

I began my story with one of my father's random facts, so perhaps it's appropriate that I end it with one. In the rolling hills of the Greater Caucasus Mountains, there's a tiny, secluded Russian village where every able man and woman can walk on tightropes. The tradition dates back more than a century. No one knows why they do it; they just do.

I once found this amusing, even ridiculous, until I considered the complexity of the lives we lead and realized we're not so different. Everyone I know walks a tightrope, including me. But, as my story shows, I'm one of the lucky ones. I had someone there to catch me when I fell.

Christmas was more than I'd hoped for. It was more than I could have hoped for. It was wonderfully nourishing to be surrounded by family again.

Justin's family was gracious and fun. In a way, Justin's father reminded me of my own: quiet, thoughtful, attentive. Only he was a plumber and my dad was a fighter pilot, so, not quite the same thing.

I have almost no memory of my mother, so having Carol, Justin's mom, around was a bit of a novelty. A wonderful one. I wasn't surprised to learn that she and Michelle had been close. In fact, they played pickleball together whenever they visited. Sounds like something Michelle would do.

As Justin had told me, his family followed the Swedish Christmas tradition of opening their gifts on Christmas Eve. I sat with the Ek family around their tree while the children—Audra's two kids and Olivia—opened their presents from *Tomten*, the Swedish Father Christmas. Watching Olivia brought back many fond memories of Michelle. It was liberating to let those memories breathe again.

Justin had set aside a present for me to give Olivia—the unicorn-mermaid we'd bought together in Salt Lake, which Olivia was pretty much over the moon about.

Unbeknownst to Justin, I had a gift for her as well. I gave Olivia her mother's opal. "This was your mommy's," I told her. "She would want you to have it. But your daddy will keep it for you until you're a little older." Justin, emotional, leaned over and kissed me.

To my surprise, Justin had a present for me. It was a beautiful gold rope bracelet. I told him I was embarrassed that I didn't have anything for him. He just said, "You're here. You couldn't have given me anything better."

After the gifts were opened, we gathered in the dining room for the *Julbord*, which, in Swedish, means Christmas

Table. It was an extravagant Swedish smorgasbord. I had my first Pepperkaker cookie, and Justin showed me how to properly break it to ensure a lifetime of love.

While we were eating, Justin's brother, Liam, filled me in on how the DEA had gone after Amelia and Guy, and how Guy, in Liam's words, "squealed like a stuck pig" after he was caught. Halfway through the story, Carol stopped him, scolding Liam for telling that kind of story on Christmas Eve. She apologized profusely, but I felt nothing but gratitude.

After dinner the adults sat in the living room and drank—no surprise—eggnog and talked. The siblings took turns telling me stories meant to embarrass Justin. I think it's a familial rite of passage.

At one point in the evening, his younger sister, Kayla, slipped and called me Michelle. For a second everyone froze. I just smiled at her and said, "Thank you," and the conversation went on as it should have.

Throughout the entire celebration, Olivia rarely left my side. At times it almost felt like she'd forgotten that I wasn't her mother and she was catching me up on all I'd missed in the last year.

The opal dream stopped happening. I kind of hoped I could have it just one last time, but with a happy ending—one where I found the gems. But no matter. What's important is what I've learned to value in the waking world.

I flew home on New Year's Day, to go back to work. In spite of everything that had happened, it was good to be back and needed. From then on, Justin and I took turns traveling each week to see each other until we finally tired of the routine and just got married.

It was a small wedding, held in Justin's parents' home and attended by Justin's family and a few of his parents' friends. I joked with Justin that we could save money by using his previous wedding photographs, since no one would be able to tell the difference anyway. He smiled and said, "We would."

We left Olivia with her grandparents and flew to Milan for our honeymoon. Justin took me to the place where Michelle had once worked. Several of her former colleagues kissed me on the cheek and welcomed me back. I didn't correct them.

We've since moved back to my father's home in Utah. Olivia sleeps in her mother's childhood bedroom. I think Michelle would have liked that.

Justin took an engineering job at the University of Utah Research Center. He also teaches at the university on the side. I guess there's a place for rocket scientists in Utah after all.

Michelle rarely took pictures—she claimed they stole the soul—and, in her case, she was right. Taking pictures changed her from a player to a spectator, and Michelle was never one to sit on the sidelines. Fortunately our father didn't share her sentiment and had boxes of photographs of Michelle and me growing up.

Olivia and I started making a scrapbook about her mom. I found that while going through the photographs Olivia couldn't always tell the difference between Michelle and me. I think, in a way, that was comforting for her. When I look at Olivia I see my sister. And that's comforting too.

Whenever I pointed out to Olivia which one of us was her

mother, I didn't feel bad at all when I said, "She was the fun one."

Michelle left me one other great gift. Eight months after Justin and I were married I learned that I was unable to bear children. In this way, Michelle gave me my greatest wish. I love Olivia as my own.

I talk to Michelle now and then. Especially about raising Olivia. I don't know if she's listening or how that all works, but there are times that I feel she's with me. But whether she is or not doesn't really matter. She's there in my heart, and that's enough.

My love for Justin continues to grow. At times, I still wonder if Michelle engineered all this. Maybe. Maybe not. I'll never know. But that Chinese proverb my father taught me still haunts me: An invisible thread connects those who are destined to meet, regardless of time, place, and circumstance. The thread may stretch or tangle, but it will never break.

A year after Justin and I were married, I finished my first book, *The Prodigal Daughter*. I've heard authors say that the book they started wasn't the one they finished. I now understand. My book is not at all what I thought I was writing. Same book, different story. I suppose the same could be said of me.

I said earlier that there were two things that people miss in the prodigal son story, but there's really three. The third is the meaning of the story itself.

The story of the prodigal son isn't really about the "lost" son at all. An author might say that the wayward son was only a literary device to share a much deeper perspective and meaning. The story was about the older brother—the one who wouldn't forgive or accept his prodigal sibling.

We know this because of who the story was told to. The teacher wasn't sharing the story with the lost—the prostitutes, thieves, and tax collectors who humbly followed him from town to town—he was telling the story to the Pharisees: self-righteous, proud, and judgmental people who looked down on others. People like me.

He was trying to teach them to look past their pride and into their hearts—to embrace the lost not with judgment or condemnation but with celebration. He was teaching them to love the wayward. For in the eyes of heaven, we are all wayward. And we are all lost. But we are never forgotten. And if there's a promise of Christmas, it couldn't be anything more than that.

ACKNOWLEDGMENTS

I wish to convey my heartfelt gratitude to all those involved in the production of this book, especially my friends at Gallery: Jennifer Bergstrom, Aimee Bell, Jennifer Long, and the rest of the crew; my long-suffering editor, Hannah Braaten; Andrew Nguyen; and my new publicist, Lauren Truskowski.

My agent, Laurie Liss, and my fabulous assistant, Diane Glad.

Thank you to my friend, advocate, and hero, Jonathan Karp. Forty-six and counting, my friend. (Books, not years!)

To my two daughters, Allyson and McKenna, who have shown me how much our medical professionals personally sacrifice to take care of the rest of us. To all the medical professionals reading this book, I hope you feel my admiration and gratitude.

And, always, my stem, Keri Lyn.

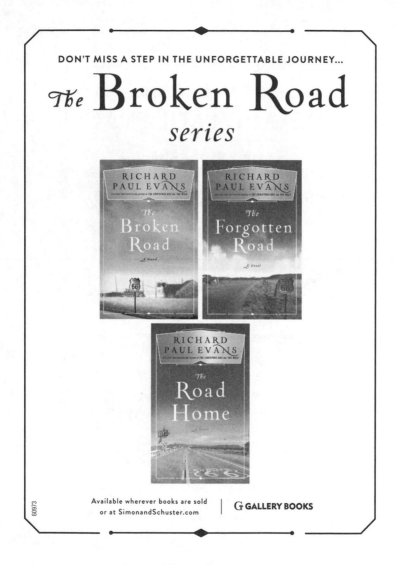